TURNING OVER MY SOUL

TURNING OVER MY SOUL

Steffin Michial McNeill

Sherena Wilkens,
Thanks for the support
& love!
Steffin

iUniverse, Inc.
New York Lincoln Shanghai

TURNING OVER MY SOUL

Copyright © 2005 by Steffin Michial McNeill

iUniverse books may be ordered through booksellers or by contacting:

iUniverse
2021 Pine Lake Road, Suite 100
Lincoln, NE 68512
www.iuniverse.com
1-800-Authors (1-800-288-4677)

ISBN-13: 978-0-595-36941-6 (pbk)
ISBN-13: 978-0-595-81350-6 (ebk)
ISBN-10: 0-595-36941-3 (pbk)
ISBN-10: 0-595-81350-X (ebk)

Printed in the United States of America

This book is dedicated in memory of
Ms. Larah Bristow
James Wells Jr.
Simeon B. Cole
You're gone, but not forgotten. I miss you so much.

ACKNOWLEDGEMENTS

*F*irst and foremost, I want to give all my praises to God, for allowing and inspiring me to write this book.

*S*econdly, I want to say, "Thank you mama," Ms. Jessie Goodall, for making me into what I am today. My Aunt, Mary Bristow, got nuthin but mad luv for ya! My sisters, Larah Andrus, Janice Whitten, and Vanessa Jackson, thanks for being proud of me. My brothers, Rev. John, and Terry McNeill. My cousins, the Bristow's and the Watson's Clan, (too many to mention by name). All my nieces and nephews, y'all stop runnin me crazy. Johnny, Barbara, and Karen Robertson, you know I luv ya!

*N*ow for the crazy people that keeps balance in my life, my friends. Betty and Val, keep on keeping on. Alvin and Al, you guys got it goin on. Dwayne, the best is yet to come. Rick, it ain't as hard as you think. Deanthony and Sam, have we been friends too long? Cornelius, don't be surprised! TC and Stacey, you still makin me laugh. Edward Law, ain't nuthin ever gonna change. Gary, we have to keep on steppin. Bishop Prince, God ain't through with you yet. Verlin, Can't nuthin come between us. M.A.B, thanks for keepin me grounded; you know you have my heart and soul. The Lee Memorial and Fair Promise AME family, thanks for all your blessings. Now for all the people I forgot, please blame it to my head and not to my heart. I luv Ya!!

CHAPTER 1

It was a hot sunny day in June 1931, I think. I was outside digging in the field, when something caught my attention. I looked up and saw this shadow coming down the dirt road toward our house. I had to put my hand up to my eyes to shield the sun. Mind you, our house is really far back into the woods. We lived in Topeka, Georgia and the houses are not close at all. It's a good mile to the next neighbor. So whomever was coming was either lost or was in trouble needing mama's help. As the shadow got closer, I could tell it was a woman from the way she was rocking from side to side. The closer she got I could tell it was a big woman, I mean a really big woman. She walked over to where I was and came right up on me and stared at my face for what seemed like a long time, and said, "I know you can't be Jimmy? I just know you can't be my little Jimmy!"

I stepped back because this big woman was scaring me.

"Yes ma'am I am, who's you?"

"Baby, I haven't seen you since you were about three," then she took a step back and got a good look at me and yelled,

"Boy, I'm your A_nt Hattie!"

She just started laughing, bouncing up and down and then yelled,

"Boy, come and give your A_nt Hattie a hug!"

She sat her two bags and a sachet down on the ground and grabbed me before I could move back and started squeezing the life out of me. Mind you, this is the biggest woman I have ever seen in my life, and I have no idea who she is!

All of a sudden, mama busted through the screen door and stood out on the porch and yelled, "Hattie, Hattie Mae, I know that can't be you! Why didn't you let me know you were coming?"

Now this Hattie, she looks like a strange one to me. I stood back to really get a good look at her. She's the biggest, blackest woman I've ever laid eyes on. She wasn't ugly she was just. I guess she would've been kinda nice looking if you squint your eyes real tight, and I mean you'll have to do it real tight.

Mama looked over at me and said "Jimmy, go take your A_nt Hattie's bags in the house."

Mama and A_nt Hattie hugged each other for a long time. Now for them to be sisters, they looked nuthin alike. I've never heard mama speak of a sister named Hattie.

My mom stepped back looking Hattie over and said, "Hattie, come on in this house girl and get out this hot sun fore you have a heat stroke. You look like you don put on a little weight."

I looked at mama and started to laugh saying to myself, "A little weight?"

A_nt Hattie wobbled up the steps taking them one at a time while mama and me stood back waiting. She got up to the top step and stood on the porch and looked back at us and said, "Whew girl, this weight is just too much to carry!"

She went into the house and looked around as if it was her first time being there.

Mama looked over to me and said, "Boy, go get your A_nt Hattie a cold glass of water, I know she's got to be hot and thirsty after walking all the way out here."

I ran into the kitchen and found the biggest jar we had, because A_nt Hattie was sho nuff a big woman. I filled the jar all the way to the top and brought the water back to her. She drank all the water in one gulp and let out the loudest burp. I couldn't help but laugh.

She looked over at me, then back at mama and said, "Pearlie, that Jimmy of yours sho has grown. He's nearly a man. Ain't seen that boy since he was a baby. He's sho nuff a handsome little man."

My mom looked back at A_nt Hattie and asked, "Hattie Mae, where's your Josiah, he didn't come with you on this trip?"

A_nt Hattie spoke in a loud voice and said, "Pearlie, that Josiah was no good! No good a tall! That man started trying to beat me! Yeap, tried to beat me till he nearly killed me! Just started beating me all the time for no reason like it was his job to do!"

Then she leaned over and whispered, "Pearlie, I had to kill him, that's the reason I'm here. I'm running from the law and need to stay here for awhile until things cool down."

I looked up at her and stepped back because I couldn't believe this woman done killed somebody. I couldn't hear whom she said she had killed but I know mama couldn't let her stay with us knowing this. Suppose if she try to kill me?

I couldn't imagine anybody trying to fight this big woman, and I don heard her say she don killed a man. Ain't nobody that crazy!

Mama looked over at her and said, "Now Hattie, you got to stop all this killing and all. You just can't go around killing everybody that gets in your way. Then you come here running from the law, that just ain't right. Lord! I hope you ain't bringing trouble behind you. It's peaceful and quiet out here Hattie; we ain't used to a lot of mess especially with the law."

I still couldn't believe A_nt Hattie don killed a man. I know one thing for sure; she'll never have to worry about me getting in her way. I am sho nuff scared of her, especially after hearing that.

A_nt Hattie started asking mama about daddy. I knew they couldn't be all that close, because daddy's been dead since I was a little boy and ain't nobody been here but mama and me for a long time. I have never laid eyes on this A_nt Hattie before and I have never heard tales of her. This was really strange to me because ain't nobody ever come to live with us before. I was really going to keep my eyes on her. She would be talking to mama and holding her hand, then she would look over at me. Every time she looked over at me, I would turn my head. I just didn't know about this. I had a funny feeling, A_nt Hattie was bringing us nuthin but trouble. I was hoping mama wouldn't let her stay with us.

After sitting and listening to mama and A_nt Hattie talk, I went outside to sit on the porch trying to make some sense out of all this. I thought about Junior and wanted to tell him all about this. I got up and went to the screen door and hollered inside, "Mama, can I go up to Junior's?"

Mama looked over at A_nt Hattie and said, "Boy go on, but don't you be up there till dark, and I mean it Jimmy, be home fore dark! You hear me, don't you?"

"Yes ma'am, I hear you!"

I started walking up to Junior's house but I didn't get too far. I spotted Junior coming back from the store. I started running towards him yelling all out of breath, "Junior, Junior! You won't believe what just happened! This big ugly woman is coming to stay with us. Junior, she's good and ugly."

Junior started laughing really hard and said, "Who is she, where is she from? Why is she comin to live with y'all?"

I turned around and looked down toward my house and said in a low voice, "She say she's my A_nt Hattie. She's my mama sister. I ain't ever heard of her before."

"Tomorrow Junior, ask your mama can you come to my house? I want you to see her for yourself. She is really strange and guess what? She don killed a man Junior and I ain't lying! She has really killed a man! I heard her say it myself. She was telling this to my mama."

Junior just stared at me and I could tell by the way he was looking, he would be scare of meeting A_nt Hattie. We ain't never known of a woman around here to kill a man before. She must be a mean strong lady if she can kill a man.

CHAPTER 2

Nearly three months has passed since I first laid eyes on A_nt Hattie. Mama was happy she was here. Mama and her would stay up late into the night talking about the old times. I guess she made good company. As for me, I still hadn't got used to her. I still kept my eyes on her. Most of the time, all she did was stay in her room or talk to mama. She never did say much to me. She caught me coming in the house one day and said, "Come here boy."

I walked over to her and she said, "Jimmy, don't you ever go in my room or bother my stuff and I mean it! I don't want no misunderstanding from a child. Now do you hear me?"

I just stood there until I heard myself say, "Yes ma'am."

She only had to tell me once never to go in her room or bother her stuff, because once was all it took. When I walked passed her room, I would walk real fast.

One day I was walking down the hall going into the kitchen. I walked passed A_nt Hattie's room and I could hear her yelling some strange words that I didn't understand. I stopped and just stood outside her door and tried to listen, but I just couldn't make any sense out of what she was saying. I couldn't figure out whom she was talking too, but she was talking real loud and getting mad. Then all of a sudden she would stop yelling and start speaking in a normal voice real fast. After hearing that, I ran down the hall. I don't know what I would have done if she had opened that door and saw me standing there.

Another time when I was coming from outside, A_nt Hattie was sitting in the living room on the sofa. She stopped me and told me to come and sit down beside her. She started talking, "Boy, I'm comin from Louisiana, by way of New Orleans. I never had any children, and I was born and raised right here. Yeap, right here in Topeka, Georgia. Left here when I was a young girl and ain't never stepped foot back here till now. Had me a good husband by the name of Josiah. He was the one man whom I was fool enuff to fall in love with, and who was dumb enuff to try to beat me."

She looked me dead in my eyes and said, "Jimmy, I'll kill anybody who ever tries to lay a hand on me; I don't take no beatings from nobody, be it man, woman, or child!"

I looked up at her and I could tell she meant what she was saying. I knew she was not to be played with. I was too scared to ask her anything, especially about the man she had killed. I knew then that A_nt Hattie was good and crazy. That A_nt Hattie was strange enuff for all the people in Topeka.

CHAPTER 3

After a couple of months had passed, a man by the name of BoHenry started coming around for A_nt Hattie. I've seen this man walking up and down the road toward this place called the, Juke-Joint. That's a place where all the grown people go to have a good time. I heard they be drinking and dancing in there. Didn't know if that man worked there or not.

My mama used to always say, "Ain't nuthin but trouble up there in that place. That place ain't nuthin but the devil's workshop."

A_nt Hattie didn't get out much, 'cept for on the weekends. So how this man name BoHenry knew her, I just didn't know. I guess it must have been from that Juke-Joint place.

BoHenry started coming around a lot for A_nt Hattie. I knew he liked her because when he came around A_nt Hattie acted differently. She started to smile more and seemed happier.

I thought to myself, "I wondered if this man knew A_nt Hattie don killed a man? I bet you if he knew that, it would be the last I would see of him."

That BoHenry must love big women because everything about A_nt Hattie was big. When she laughed, everything on her moved. BoHenry was a little man; he was just a tad bit bigger and taller than me. Everything A_nt Hattie told BoHenry to do he did, he even did it with a smile. Now what they saw in each other, I don't know. But I know he made A_nt Hattie smiled a lot. As long as A_nt Hattie was happy, I was happy. As for me, I couldn't understand it. I just sat back, watched, and wondered.

It was unusually warm for fall. BoHenry was coming around nearly every other day for A_nt Hattie. As a matter of fact, A_nt Hattie asked me to call him Uncle BoHenry, because he was better than a husband. Every time they looked at each other, they would just smile, like they were sharing a secret. BoHenry didn't mind looking and staring at A_nt Hattie, but whenever she looked at me, I always turned my head because she was nuthin pretty to look at. Besides, I was still scared of her.

One night while I was sleeping, I heard the screen door slam. I got up and noticed A_nt Hattie going out the back door. I was wondering at this time of the night where she would be going, or what she would be doing. I looked out the back door and saw she was carrying that satchel she had the first day she arrived. I continued to watch her move through the moonlight till she disappeared into the darkness. I was too scared to call out to her or try to follow her. I just laid there trying to stay awake until she got back up to the house.

I thought to myself, "I sho hope A_nt Hattie's real careful out there, cause it's a big well down there. I would hate for her to fall in, cause as big as she is, can't nobody pull her out."

I waited for A_nt Hattie to come back up to the house for what seemed like a long time, then the next thing I know, it was daylight. I musta fell asleep.

I got up and went into the kitchen and A_nt Hattie was cookin over the stove and humming. She looked over to me and gave me the strangest look. I didn't know if A_nt Hattie knew I was scared of her or not. I didn't know how long she stayed out there last night, but she didn't look tired at all. I was wondering when she was going to go back to New Orleans, but I think A_nt Hattie was here to stay. She was getting mighty comfortable.

A_nt Hattie turned from the stove and said, "Boy, you sho nuff a nice looking young man. How old are you boy?"

I held my head down and said, "Twelve."

"Well, are you sweet on anybody yet?"

I kept my head down and said "Naw ma'am I ain't."

With her back still toward me she said, "Well you sit yourself on down so you can eat."

I guess in between all the strangeness, A_nt Hattie was trying to warm up to me. I sat down at the table and started thinking about what had happened last night. I wanted to ask her about where she was going or what she was doing outside so late. She still had her back toward me when I said, "A_nt Hattie, I got up late last night and I heard you going out the back door. Couldn't tell where you were going because it was too dark, but you were carrying that satchel with you. What were you doing out there at that time of the night?"

A_nt Hattie looked at me with those beady little eyes and said in a loud voice, "Boy! Didn't your mama teach you to mind your own business and not ask grown people about theirs? Now you just sit there and eat your food and never ask your A_nt Hattie about her business ever again! If Hattie Mae wants you to know something, then she'll tell you."

A_nt Hattie gave me the meanest look afterward.

I sat at the table with my head down because I could feel her still staring at me. I didn't want her to kill me too, so I wasn't going to say another word.

I started looking around for mama, because I didn't want to eat with A_nt Hattie all by myself. I guess she noticed me looking for mama, because she turned around toward the stove and said, "Your mama had to go into town early this mornin boy to take care of some business. She'll be back soon, so gon and eat and get out of here."

I didn't know what I was going to do if it was going to be the two of us together all day. I sat at the table scared to move and started to eat. I started hearing this strange noise coming from outside. A_nt Hattie just kept cookin and payin no attention to it. I looked up from the table and said, "A_nt Hattie, somebody is outside this house. You don't hear that noise?"

A_nt Hattie turned and looked towards the back porch and said, "Boy, that ain't nobody but BoHenry out there. He's cutting me down some herbs that I need to make my medicine with. Let me get that fool in here so he can eat his breakfast fore he messes around and hurt himself."

A_nt Hattie moved away from the stove and walked to the back door and yelled, "BoHenry, come on in now so you can eat your breakfast."

After about five minutes, BoHenry came through the back door all covered in weeds smiling at A_nt Hattie. I looked at him coming through the door and he looked at me and said, "Morning boy."

He walked over to the table and pulled out a chair and sat down. A_nt Hattie turned from the stove and looked over at him and yelled, "Now BoHenry Johnson, don't sit at my table without washin up first! I know your mama don raised you better than that. Where are your manners?"

A_nt Hattie looked up toward the ceiling and held up both hands and said, "Lord, what kind of man you don sent me? This man ain't been taught nuthin about Holiness."

I started to smile because with all that killing and meanest, A_nt Hattie don found her some religion.

CHAPTER 4

A_nt Hattie did everything she could to fit in. She started trying to go to church, but I think she didn't like it much. When we were walking downtown everybody stared and talked about her behind her back. They were wondering who she was and where she was from. She said she didn't see too many of the old faces she remembered when she used to live here. I know those people didn't know what I knew about A_nt Hattie, because if they did, they would leave her be. Wouldn't even look in her direction.

Everywhere A_nt Hattie went, BoHenry would be there walking bout two steps behind her. A_nt Hattie walked really fast everywhere she went. BoHenry had a hard time keeping up with her because his steps were too short.

One day while we were walking home from the store, he just got tired and yelled out!

"Now Hattie, why you have to walk so fast? You know I can't keep up with you walkin like that. My legs ain't as long as yours. Now you gots to slow down!"

A_nt Hattie turned around and pulled a rag from her pocket and wiped her forehead. Then she put her hands on her hips and said, "BoHenry, it's too hot out here to be trying to walk slow! Now you know I can't stand too much heat! Lord knows I can't stand it! Now you gonna have to try to walk faster or just start runnin. You make the choice!"

After she said that, she just turned around and started walking back at the same pace. I started to laugh because of the look on Bo Henry's face. I knew if he thought he could beat A_nt Hattie, I think he would have tried right then and there.

We finally got to the house and A_nt Hattie came through the door with sweat running all off her face. She was nothing pretty to look at. I had already sat down on the couch when she came in. She looked over to me and gave me the meanest look and told me to gon and get her some water in that jar of hers.

I asked BoHenry if he wanted some water as well. A_nt Hattie gave me that mean look again and said, "Boy, you know my Bo wants some water, ain't he been out there walking too? Ain't you learnt nuthin bout how to treat people?"

I got up and went into the kitchen, when I noticed mama sitting in the back bedroom folding some clothes. I bought the water back to A_nt Hattie in her big ole jar and gave Uncle Bo a smaller one. A_nt Hattie looked over to me and said, "Gon on back there boy and see where your mama's at. I needs to talk to her."

"She's back there in the back bedroom, A_nt Hattie. I saw her on my way into the kitchen."

A_nt Hattie tried to get up off the couch but she couldn't. She started rocking back and forth trying to get up. She kept rockin and getting frustrated using one hand on the back of the sofa to push off of. She finally got up and started walking down the hall pulling down her dress behind her. I walked behind her until she entered the room and stopped at the doorway. Mama turned around and saw A_nt Hattie standing behind her. She turned back around and continued folding clothes and said, "Hattie Mae, I went into town today and some man was asking around bout you."

A_nt Hattie looked surprise and said "Asking bout me? Now don't nobody know me here in this town. Who could this be asking bout me?"

Mama turned back around and looked at A_nt Hattie and said "I don't have any ideal Hattie; just thought I'll let you know, that's all."

A_nt Hattie turned around and started out the door and said, "Hum, that's strange."

CHAPTER 5

My name is BoHenry Johnson and I was born in Tulsa, Oklahoma. My mama passed away at an early age leaving my aunt to raise me. I am the middle of seven children, three brothers on one side and three sisters on the other. I never knew anything about my daddy. When I came of age, all I could think about was getting away. I hated living in Oklahoma. It was boring, and everybody stayed in your business. I had heard many things about Chicago. That there were lots of jobs, and plenty of beautiful women. So as soon as I got old enough and saved enough money, I headed up north. I hadn't been home or seen my family since. I had been gone so long, I had actually forgotten how long. I was always longing to see them, but time just got away. I especially missed my youngest sister JaniceSandra, because we were really close.

I have always thought of myself as a smart man, but sometimes I just made dumb decisions. I went into the big city searching for my dream, which is exactly what I found. I met the love of my life and her name was Sophie.

One afternoon I had to run an errand for my boss. I hated going into this one section of town called the Avenue. Always having to see those women walking up and down the street with little or no clothes on, asking for money to do this and to do that. But I had to come through here anyway. I knew I was shy, always has been and probably always will be. Every time I passed through this section of town, I would always put my head down and walk really fast. Some of the women found it funny when they would call out to me, "Hey little man, I can sho nuff make you feel big! You want to have a date with me mister big stuff!" Then they would just bust out laughing. I walked as fast as I could until I couldn't hear or see them anymore. Once I got passed that area, I would hold my head up and slow my walking.

On this one particular day, it was very hot and the sun was shining bright. I had just passed through the Avenue. I slowed my walk when something caught my eye. I couldn't believe it! I had never seen such a beautiful and classy woman like the one I was seeing right now. I couldn't even look directly at her, but at the same time I couldn't take my eyes off her. She was more than beautiful; she was an angel from heaven. When I eventually passed her, she was staring at me. I continued walking with my head turned backward staring at her. When she was out of my sight, I thought about turning around to try to meet her, at least get her name. I knew I was running an errand and needed to get where I was going. I thought she might be out of my league, but I knew I needed to see her again. I would do just about anything to get her attention.

While I was walking, I couldn't take my mind off of what had just happened. I started thinking about how I could get somebody like that. I knew the first thing I would need to do and that would be to get a better job. I had to impress this woman.

I started thinking, "What type of good job could I get? I hadn't finish school."

I always knew I could make it in Chicago. They treated colored people different here than in the south. I knew one thing for sure that would impress this woman and that was having a lot of money. I could tell a woman like that loved money. She needed to buy nice things, and nice things cost money. I know a woman like that would love a man that carried a lot of money. I thought about the one skill that always got me fast money, but it came with lots of problems. That was gambling. Now I knew I hadn't really gambled in a long time and maybe I had lost my skills, but I had to try anything.

My cousins, who were much older, but I was much wiser, always tried to take my money. That's what turned me into a good gambler. I got tired of them always taking my money. The first thing I had to do was find out where the gambling took place and how to get in on it. I knew gambling was illegal but the law didn't really care about it too much. Everybody who could do it was doing it. It wasn't a big crime.

As time passed, I kept my eyes and ears opened. I knew I had to stick to my plan. I had heard about this poolroom about three blocks from where I lived. I had to get a job working there because I heard gambling took place in the back room.

One day, I decided to go and talk to the owner. I found out the only job he had, was keeping the place clean. I took the job and did the best I could. The boss man liked me and saw I was a hard worker. As time grew, the boss man knew I could be trusted and started leaving me in charge of everything. He would just take off in the middle of the day and wouldn't come back. Every now and then I would go in the backroom and watch the men gamble. I would watch them real carefully. I knew the ones who was good at gambling and the ones who were just fools losing their money. Some of the gamblers were young and old, black and white, tryin to make their paychecks grow. They would always ask me to come in on some of the games after I had gotten paid on Friday and teased me because I was from down south. They started calling me "Bama." They thought I didn't know anything about gambling or the city life. I started waiting my time.

Once I knew everything about running the poolroom, and seeing who was cheating and who was okay, I finally ask if I could get in on some of the games. I was a little nervous at first, and losing nearly my whole paycheck, but with time my old skills came back to me and I started winning. I started winning a lot. The word got around the streets that I was a good gambler, and I was the man to beat. With the word going out about me, everybody started treating me differently. Everybody knew I was making lots of money from gambling. I wanted to change my look. Looked like I was somebody. I didn't know much about dressing, but I was going to show that woman that I was worthy of her attention. I started buying new clothes and dressing nice every day. People started to respect me more. I knew I needed a woman on my arm that could perhaps teach me some things, and make me feel more like a man. It had been a long time since I had been with a woman. And the only woman I had eyes for, was the angel that I saw while I was walking.

CHAPTER 6

My name is Sophie Lavon Williams. I was born and raised on the Southside of Chicago. I was taken out of school at an early age, because my mama needed me at home to take care of my brothers. I have eight brothers under me. I'm the oldest. Each and every one of us has different fathers. My mama has no ideal who or where the fathers were.

At an early age, mama started noticing how beautiful I was gettin and how men started payin attention to me. I was already taller than she was and had always been thin. My body was really fillin out and my skin was nice. She started gettin jealous of me as the years grew. She started beatin me for no reason and always called me out my name, makin me feel as if I was worth nuthin. I practically raised those boys all by myself. I did all the cookin, cleanin, ironin and washin, because my mama never had time. She always had men in the house. They were sittin around drinkin beer with loud music playin all times of the night. All I ever had on my mind was gettin the hell out of that house. I hated being there. It was never any peace and quiet. I was never gonna be like my mama, having all those men runnin in and out all times of the mornin. I could tell mama didn't like me and I didn't like her much either. I wanted to make sumethin out of my life, but I didn't get too much schoolin. I loved my brothers and would do anything for them. We always stuck together. They were all the family I had. I was determined to do sumethin other than have a house full of babies and not know who the daddies were.

I used to find old magazines and look through them. I would walk downtown looking through the department store windows wishin, I could be in some other place at some other time. I would watch the other girls my age in their school clothes carryin books, with handsome young men walkin beside them. They would look at me and turned their nose up, or start laughin when they got close to me. I hated them and wished I had that type of lifestyle.

I had always wanted to go to school to be with people my own age, but my mama kept me at home. I knew I could never be one of them. The older I got, the more responsibilities she put on me. The more responsibilities, the more I hated her.

Men were always comin around asking bout me. Asking my mama, "When is that girl of yours going to be old enough to take the company of a man?"

My mama always laughed it off, but it made her even more jealous.

Once I got of age, I realized I had sumethin a lot of men kept asking for. I watched my mama deal with the men that came callin, so I knew what they were after. I figured I would not just give it away, that there was a price that came with it. Men would always tell me how beautiful I was. I knew men like women with fair skin, long hair, and a beautiful body. Also men were willing to pay whatever price I asked for, just to be in my company. By me having so many brothers, I knew how to set a man straight and how to take care of myself. If I was ever going to get out of my mama's house and stay out, then I would have to use my body and looks to get me through life. I watched how other people act, and knew I needed a plan. A plan that would get me out into the world to see some things, perhaps be loved by a real man. But most of all, all I wanted was to learn how to read, write, and be like people my own age.

CHAPTER 7

I felt my gambling and working in the poolroom was making me a decent living. I knew it was time to find out who this woman was, that I passed on the street. I just couldn't get her off my mind. I had not seen her since the first day I laid eyes on her. I walked around town several times trying to find out who she was and where she worked or how she spent her time. I asked everybody I knew about her. Most of the men I asked said she only wanted to use them for their money. I couldn't understand why they only had bad things to say about her.

From asking so many people, I finally found out her name was Sophie. I wasn't going to believe anything bad about my angel. I knew they had tried to get with her and she wouldn't give them the time of day. She was too classy for them any way, so they were just trying to put her down. I didn't drink so I had no use to hang out in the bars or in the club and that's where I heard my angel spent most of her time. I knew the word had gotten out about me, about how good of a gambler I was, and I carried plenty of money.

I had heard around town bout this man named Bo. I didn't know who he was, or where he came from, but I knew I had to find out. I was going to do whatever it took to meet him. Anybody who carried that much money, I needed to know.

Now I knew the best way to get a man and his money was after he had gotten drunk. Somebody had pointed Bo out to me one day and I watched him until he disappeared around the corner. I couldn't remember ever seeing him in any bars, or any other places I knew of. I heard he worked at the poolroom but women weren't allowed to go in there. I knew I had to get him, be in the same place at the same time. I needed a plan.

One afternoon, I was walking downtown toward Sears and Roebuck when I spotted my angel looking through one of the department store windows. I knew this was my opportunity to meet her. I couldn't believe my chance had finally come. The closer I got to her, the more nervous I got. I got close enough to notice how radiant and beautiful she really was. I could smell the scent of her sweet perfume in the air. I knew she had to become my woman. And whatever it would take to get her, I was willing to do. I couldn't believe my luck was this good.

I walked up to my angel and said, "Hum Scuse me,"

She continued to look into the department store window ignoring me.

"Scuse me," I said again.

She turned around and looked at me and didn't say a word. She just stared at me. I knew I wasn't a bad looking man. I figured I was kinda handsome for a short, light skinned man with short black curly hair with a small mole on the right side of my nose.

I looked right into her eyes and said, "My name is Bo, BoHenry Johnson.

She turned and looked through the window then back at me.

"Well, well, if it ain't the Mr. BoHenry I've heard so much about around town. It's a pleasure to meet you. My name is Sophie, Sophie Lavon Williams."

I knew I had a lot to say to my angel, but nuthin would come to my mind. Even as my mouth moved, no sound would come out.

Sophie kept staring at me and asked, "Well, ain't you gonna say something?"

I knew I was shy, but this was my opportunity to get to know my angel. I was really nervous.

"How do you do, Ms. Sophie?"

"Well that's more like it, and I be doin just fine thank you."

I was wondering what it was that Sophie had heard about me. I started to stare into the department store window, keeping my head down and my eyes away from hers. This was my opportunity to ask her out, but I knew she was too sophisticated to go out on a date with somebody like me. I glanced over at her. I wanted to say something but the words wouldn't come out. I was confused, and didn't know what to do.

I turned and looked at her and stared. I could feel my mouth moving, but I didn't know what I was saying. Then I jump when I heard her say, "Dinner! Are you asking me out on a date BoHenry?"

I didn't know what had happened. I knew I was thinking it but I didn't know I was saying it.

I looked away and said, "Yea, I guess I am askin you out on a date."

I started sweatin, knowin she was lookin at me like I don lost my mind. I knew a woman like this would never give me the time of day. Then I heard her say, "Yea, I don't mind havin dinner with ya."

I was really caught by surprise and said "Well, what about Friday night around seven?"

I thought about what Bo had asked me. I knew on Friday night and the weekend is when I made most of my money. That's when most of the men I dealt with got paid. I knew I had to give Bo an off night, like a weekday.

"I have plans for this Friday; but perhaps we can go on Monday evening if that's good with you."

I started to smile at Sophie, because all I needed was one chance to make it with her. I wanted her to be mine. I just couldn't believe how beautiful she was. This was more than a dream come true.

I looked at her with a big smile on my face and said, "Ms. Sophie, you have got yourself a date."

She smiled and said, "I thought I told you to call me Sophie. Ms, is my mama's name."

CHAPTER 8

I was happy everyday thinking about my date with Sophie. I had been renting a room in a boarding house and knew it was time to start thinking about finding a real place to live. I thought it would be nice to have a dream house for Sophie and me. Sophie was all I had on my mind since meeting her. I would wake up in the morning thinking bout her, and when I went to sleep at night, she would still be there. This angel had some type of spell over me. Whatever it took to get this woman, I was going to do it. It had been a long time since a woman had caught my interest like this. I knew I had to get myself together. Act like I was sharp. I wanted Sophie to think I was special.

I told everybody at the poolroom about my date. Most of the men there said I was only asking for nuthin but trouble with that girl. That she was not the type of girl you would take on a date. I knew they were jealous of me. I had already taken all their money. Now I'm going on a date with the prettiest girl in town. What more could I want?

CHAPTER 9

My name is Ms Tiddle Mae Stevens and I run the Boarding house over on Main Street. I knew everybody business before it happened. I wasn't nosey, I was just cautious because it's best to be safe than sorry. I always kept my eyes on Bo. He was one of my best customers. I knew he was a hard worker and an honest man. He had never been a day late with the rent. I wasn't ever going to let anything happen to him.

I had made it up in my mind the first day I laid eyes on Bo that I was going to look out for him. He's a country boy and I don't want nobody trying to take advantage of him. I told him that any type of dealings he made, to make sure he come and talk to me bout it first.

One evening, I was washing down the hallway, and Bo was coming in from work. I had noticed all week he was acting all strange-like, so I asked him, "BoHenry Johnson, what in the world is wrong with you here lately boy?"

He looked up at me with a shy grin on his face.

"Ms. Tiddle Mae, my life has changed for the better. I don met me a woman. Yeap I sho have."

I stared at him and asked, "Who is this woman and what is her name that got you jumping and grinning so?"

"Now Ms. Tiddle Mae, I've been trying for months to meet this woman and ask her out, and I finally got the nerves to do just that. I still can't believe it. Her name is Ms. Sophie Williams."

My eyes got big as marbles and my voice got raspy like Satan and said, "I know you are not talking about Sophie, Florence Jean's girl? The one who lives over by the tracks on Washington Avenue? Is that the Sophie you're talking about?"

"Well, now Ms. Tiddle Mae I haven't had a chance to find out where she lives just yet, but I know she's the prettiest thing I've ever laid eyes on."

I looked Bo straight in the eyes and said, "Lord boy, what you don got yourself into?"

I started thinking, "Everybody in town knew about Sophie, and knew what type of work she did. They knew she used men to get what she wanted. I've known that girl since the day she was born, and knew she was nuthin but trouble."

I looked at Bo again and said, "Boy do you hear me talking to you? I asked you, what have you don got yourself into?"

He looked at me kind of strange and asked, "Ms. Tiddle Mae, what do you mean, what I don got myself into? We ain't doin nuthin but goin out to eat. That can't be getting into too much of anything."

He held his head down and said, "I've just met her and I know I can love me a woman like that. She is just what I need in my life. I think we could make each other happy"

I started thinking bout what Bo had said and knew I would have to go and talk to Sophie. Bo don't need no nasty ole woman like her around him. He needs a church going woman, a woman who would appreciate him and treat him right. I'm going to make sure that's exactly what he finds, even if I have to find her myself. I made a promise to make it my business to watch over Bo, and Lord, that is what I'm gonna do!

I was still standing there trying to figure out what I was going to do about all this when I noticed Bo had walked down the hall going into his room.

The next morning I got up early to straighten out that Sophie. I couldn't sleep a wink after hearing Bo talk about her. I ain't never seen a man so strung out over a woman before in all my days. Like she's the last woman on earth. How dare her try to wrap her nasty little fingers around my Bo. I headed up toward Sophie's house over on Washington Ave. When I got there, I noticed somebody coming down the steps. I couldn't see exactly who it was, so I walked a little faster to get a better look. When I got close enough, I noticed coming down the steps was Ms. Nasty herself. I walked faster so I could talk to her before she got to the bottom of the steps.

When I got up to her, I looked her straight in the eyes and said, "Hello Sophie."

She looked at me and said, "Good Morning Ms Tiddle Mae, how are you?"

She continued to walk down the steps but stopped when I said, "Well, I'm not doing so well. I want to ask you something about what's troubling me."

"Troubling you? Now how can I help you with something that's troubling you?"

I moved up to the same step Sophie was standing on and looked her eye to eye like the good Christian woman I am. I am not that tall and kind of stout in built, but I can handle myself pretty well.

"Well, now you just listen to me."

I guess I must have caught her off guard because she looked at me as if I had lost my mind.

"Ms. Tiddle Mae, you got something you would like to say to me?"

I cleared my throat and said, "Yes, I would like to ask you something. Now what is this, BoHenry Johnson is telling me about you and him trying to get something started?"

She looked at me like she didn't know what I was talking about, so I continued talking.

"Sophie, I want you to listen and listen to me good. There is no way on this earth I will let you get your hands on my Bo. Bo is a good man and he doesn't know what type of woman you are."

Sophie stood with her hands on her hips.

"Ms. Tiddle Mae, you need to mind your own business because this does not concern you at all. Bo is a grown man and I am a grown woman. I am sure we can make our own decisions. Look at me."

She waved her hands over her body and posed.

"You know it's hard for a man not to like what he sees unless sumethin is the matter with em. Bo likes me and I know he carries plenty of money. I ain't the only woman who's tryin to get with Bo. He came to me, I didn't come to him. Now if you are havin a problem with that, you need to talk to him. Besides, I needs me a man like that. A man who can take some of this pressure off my back. Lord knows I need some relief. But like I said, we are both grown. He doesn't need no old meddling fool like you trying to be his mama."

After listening to what she had just said I took in a deep breath, because I couldn't believe this girl was this bold to be talking to me any ole kind of way. This has really sent me back to my old ways. Apparently she has forgotten that I am an upstanding Christian woman, and a pillar in the community. Has she forgotten who I am and what I stand for? She just can't talk to me like this. Apparently she has lost her mind.

I got closer to Sophie's face to make sure she heard me and heard me good.

"Girl, if you think I don't know what you are out here doing, then you must be the fool. Does Bo know you are out here in these streets ho'in? Selling your body for a piece of change that still won't make your ends meet. Ain't that what they call it, ho'in? Huh? What do you think that man is going to think of you when he finds out that you ain't nuthin but a two-penny ho? Now I'm a good upstanding Christian woman and I ain't lost my religion in a long time. Nobody has gotten to me like you have gotten to me this morning. Unless it was way before I gave my life over to the Lord, before I got saved. I want you to listen, and listen to me good so there would be no misunderstanding about what I'm saying. Now since your mouth has wrote a check your ass can't cash, we will see if he still wants to get to know you or be with you after I put my two cents in it. Don't you think that when somebody sees you two together, they're going to tell him about you? You are too well known around here in these parts to try to hide something like that. When I get back up there to that Boarding House, I'm going to have a little talk with Mister Bo."

I thought about what Ms. Tiddle Mae was saying and knew she was right. I had forgotten all about my lifestyle when I met Bo. I didn't know what I was going to do. I knew I had to tell him sumethin because it would surely get back to him. I really did liked Bo. I knew he was the type of man who would go out of his way to take care of me. That was exactly the type of man I needed. I knew this was gonna stay on my mind all day, so I would have to talk Ms. Tiddle Mae out of tellin him. I needed a plan.

I started looking sad and held my head down and said, "Ms. Tiddle Mae, I am sorry about what I have just said to you. It was mean and disrespectful. You are right, Bo is a good man but Ms. Tiddle Mae I'm not a bad person. Just have to do what I have to, to survive. You have known me all my life. You know my mama and what type of life I've had. I don't want to be nuthin like her havin all those babies by different men. Bo may be my ticket to a better life! I don't want much; I just want a real chance at life. I have never had a chance for a real life. I will tell Bo everything about me on Monday, when we have our date. Please don't say anythin to him just yet. Please give me a chance to tell him. I promise, I will come back and tell you when I have told him everything. Please! Just give me a chance."

I started feeling sorry for Sophie. I knew exactly what she was talking about. I had always liked Sophie and felt she was too beautiful of a girl to be doing what she does. Whenever we would pass on the streets, she would always be pleasant. She would always smile and speak. I didn't like what she was doing, but she was always nice. Never disrespected me a day in her life 'cept for right now. I had always tried to get Florence Jean to send those children to school. I knew most of those boys were over there just waiting to go to jail. They mama ain't taught them a damn thing! They were nuthin but trouble!

I knew Sophie was right. It wasn't her fault how she was raised. But with no education and no family, I guess she's doing the best she can. Lord knows she's surviving.

I looked Sophie dead in the eyes and said, "Alright Sophie, I won't say nuthin to BoHenry, but you better tell him what he is getting himself into and I mean you better tell him soon. You just can't go around fooling people pretending to be something you're not, and the next time, you need to mind your place and your manners. Don't let me have to lose my religion on your again. I expect for you to be telling me something by some time next week. I mean it too! Don't let me have to end up telling Bo about you because if I do, I don't have nuthin nice to say. Last but not least. Don't let me have to come over here again because if I do, I ain't bringing my religion with me."

CHAPTER 10

I couldn't wait for Monday to come so I could go out on my date with Sophie. I had been looking forward to this day every since I laid eyes on her. I started getting dressed early in the day. I wanted everything to be perfect. I already had my shoes shined and my haircut, so I didn't have much to do. I had seen Sophie only once doing the week to ask her about where she lived and where we were going to meet up.

I started walking to the restaurant at about six thirty, so we could have a good table. The restaurant wasn't too crowded but it was very noisy. I wasn't used to going to restaurants so I guess they were all noisy like this. I just wanted this to be a special night that's all. I had to impress this woman so she can like me. I waited for Sophie for what seemed like hours. I finally saw her walk into the restaurant and she was the perfect vision of beauty. I knew I could look at this woman for the rest of my life.

Sophie looked around and saw me sitting in the back in one of the booths. She started toward me and I stood up from the table and just stared at her. I didn't know what to say. The words wouldn't come to my lips. Sophie stared into my eyes and said "Hello BoHenry, you look mighty fine tonight."

I smiled, "Sophie, I have never seen anybody as pretty as you. You are more beautiful than an angel, please sit down."

Sophie smiled and patted me on the arm.

The waiter came over and asked us what we wanted to drink. I didn't drink alcohol, but tonight was a special occasion. I looked up toward the waiter and said, "I will take a glass of red wine."

Sophie looked at me and ordered the same.

I could tell she felt this was her night as well. It seemed no man has taken such an interest in her to even take her out to a nice restaurant.

She smiled at me and I was wondering why she was smiling. "Sophie I see you are smiling. You look so happy."

She tried to cover her smile with her hand and said, "Well, this is actually the first time in my life I have gon out on a real date. This is sumethin I have always wanted to do. I just want to say, thank you Bo."

The waiter came back with the wine and asked us if we were ready to order. I had been staring at Sophie the entire evening, so I hadn't had a chance to look at the menu. I was hoping she would order for the both of us, since a lot of the things on the menu I couldn't read or recognize.

She looked over to me. I was hoping she wasn't expecting for me to read the menu to her. I looked up at the waiter and asked if he could come back later.

Sophie started looking around the restaurant and said, "Bo, this is a nice restaurant. Everybody is dressed so nice. This is more like a dream. I wished this night would last forever."

All of a sudden Sophie had this look on her face. Like something was bothering her.

"Sophie is something not right?"

She started telling me she had sumethin to talk to me about, but didn't know how to or when. The waiter came around again and asked us if we were ready to order. I asked the waiter what he recommended. We both ordered catfish.

As soon as the waiter left, Sophie looked over at me and said, "BoHenry, you're a nice man, and I am having a nice time. This is the first time a man has taken an interest in me just for me. There are a lot of things you don't know bout me. I want to tell you a little bout myself before you take an interest in me."

I smiled and said, "Well Sophie, you are just a little too late for that, because I'm already interested in you. When I saw you for the first time, I knew I wanted you to be in my life."

Sophie cut me off and said, "Now BoHenry, let me say what is on my mind before I get too nervous and can't say it."

She started to explain to me about her mother and how she was raised being the oldest girl with eight brothers. She explained to me about not being able to go to school and how she never learnt to read or write that well.

I was listening and hanging on to every word she was saying. I was looking at her but I didn't say anything. I was thinking about everything she was saying.

I started feeling more sorry than ashamed of her. I knew it was hard for her to survive with no education because it's not easy for me and I'm a man. I continued to listen while she was talking. I couldn't take my eyes off of her. She was so beautiful to me. I couldn't understand why a man hadn't made her his wife, to love her and to take care of her.

She continued talking when I noticed a tear starting to run down her face. She was looking so sad and pitiful that I never wanted to leave her alone.

I interrupted her and asked, "Sophie, have you ever been married?"

She looked at me surprise and said, "Bo, I am tryin to tell you why I don't have a steady man in my life. Once I got old enough I moved out on my own. I didn't have much education and didn't have any skills. I knew men were attracted to me, so I used my body and looks to get what I wanted. That's how I'm makin it through life now."

She stared at me to see what I was feeling by looking into my eyes. I didn't say anything. I just stared back at her.

I waited for her to finish talking and cleared my throat. I put my head down and said, "Sophie I don't understand how a woman can give up her body for money. You are too beautiful for that. I do understand your situation, but I can't understand that."

She reached over and touched me on the shoulder and said, "That was the only thing I knew how to do. I didn't want to do it, I had too. I didn't have to many choices in my life. I had to survive the best way I knew how."

She tried to look into my eyes, but I kept my head down. I guess she could tell I was hurting or felt deceived.

She looked over to me and said, "Bo, please try to understand what I have just said to you. I am not tryin to hurt you. I am being honest. I am the oldest of eight. My life wasn't easy. It was pure hell. I like you and I want you to like me. You are the first man who has ever taken the time to get to know me. Please try to forgive me."

I lifted my head and looked into her eyes that were still crying and said, "Sophie I have no choice but to forgive you. We all have don some things we are ashamed of. I know it wasn't easy for you to tell me this, but I preciate it. I know some people thinks that since I am from the country, I don't understand things so well, but I understand just plenty. I want you to be honest with me and I will be honest with you. From this day forward if we are to be seeing each other, then you will have to stop doing those things. I will take care of you, if that's what you need me to do."

She looked into my eyes and said, "BoHenry, this is the first time I have felt what it is like to be cared for. I am truly happy for the first time in my life."

She made up her mind that night that whatever it took to make this man happy, she was willing to do.

CHAPTER 11

I was wonderin who this was in town askin bout me. I didn't tell a soul I was comin to Georgia. I went out on the front porch and sat down in that old rockin chair on the front porch. That chair was on its last legs. I started thinkin bout things from my past. Jimmy came out on the porch and sat down on the steps. He looked up at me while I rocked back and forth. Every time I would rock, the chair would just squeak. I looked down at him and he was still starin up at me. Everything was so quiet.

After awhile, Jimmy looked up at me and said, "A_nt Hattie, I remember you tellin mama you killed your husband, how did you kill him?"

I just ignored him until he started to ask me again. I cut him off and gave him the meanest look and said, "Now Jimmy, didn't I tell you to never ask me bout my business. Boy you a child tryin to meddle in grown folks business. I will tell you again, if Hattie Mae wants you to know sumethin, then she'll tell you. Now go get a broom and start sweepin up this here porch, I just don't like no child meddlin in grown folks business. It just ain't right."

I settled back into the rockin chair and started lookin out toward the sun and said, "Lord, it sho nuff is hot, it's hot enough to fry an egg out here."

I continued rockin, and fannin myself while starin out into space. I was deep in thought about sumethin. All sorts of things were runnin through my head. I especially couldn't stop thinkin bout my Josiah. I started thinkin bout the first time we met. That Josiah was sho nuff a handsome man. Lord knows I loved me some Josiah. The first time I laid eyes on him, I was in a Blues Club. I know I was lookin good that night. Couldn't nobody dance the blues like ole Hattie. I started laughin out loud till I noticed Jimmy starin at me.

I looked over at him and went back to my thoughts.

That Josiah came up to me and asked me to dance. My first look at him, I knew he was gonna be my husband. He asked me my name and I said, "Hattie Mae."

He said it was the prettiest name he had ever heard.

He told me his name was Josiah Ray Thompson.

I asked him, "What type of name is Josiah?"

"It was my granddaddy's name."

I started to smile, and was thinkin, "That was the first time anybody had ever told me my name was pretty."

The music came on and I started swayin back and forth. Josiah asked me if I wanted to dance. Fore I had a chance to answer, he don grabbed me by the arm and led me to the dance floor and we danced the whole night. We didn't miss a song. We danced until the club closed. We were both soakin wet and my feet were killin me. I couldn't get enough of him and he seem like he couldn't get enough of Hattie.

He asked me if he could walk me home. I was nuthin but smiles cause I liked this man. All durin the walk home, he talked about being with me and how pretty I was. He acted like he didn't mind me being a little big boned or dark skinned. I could have listen to him talk all night.

No man has ever taken an interested in me like that before. This man was layin it on me strong, and I was takin it in anyway he gave it to me.

Josiah started comin around nearly every day. He started telling me bout his family. He told me he had two sisters, and he was the youngest. His sister always preached to him about how to treat a woman. They couldn't understand what he saw in me. They were teachin him a light skinned woman with good hair made the best wife, and gave you the prettiest kids. A dark woman was hardheaded and wouldn't listen to her husband, and her kids would be bad and ugly. I was just the opposite of what they wanted for Josiah.

He was really close to his sisters and I could tell he really cared what they thought. He eventually fell in love with me and wanted his sisters to at least be nice to me. But they weren't. I would see them in passin and speak. They would roll their eyes at me and not say a word, like they were better than me. So when Josiah made the announcement he was gonna marry me, his sisters tried to talk him out of it. They told him if he married me, he was only askin for trouble and they could tell I was nuthin but trouble waitin to happen. They said they would never speak to him again, nor come to the weddin.

Three months down the road, I married Josiah. I was Mrs. Hattie Mae Thompson. Everything was goin just fine. Josiah bought an old shack from some man he used to work for. He wanted it to be our home. He promised me, once we got settled we would do better and move. He started doin work around the place to make it decent, fixin little odds and ends. It wasn't a bad place to me, just needed a little work. I would've lived in a cave if it meant I was gonna be with my Josiah. I started takin in white folks laundry to help out my man. Josiah got a good job workin at the steel-mill. We were really happy together. Every now and then, we would still go to the blues club and dance the entire night. Whew! That man could still dance. That man sho loved him some Hattie Mae and I loved me some Josiah.

I remembered after a few years of livin together, I was takin in some laundry and beatin out some sheets, when a man came knockin at my door. I opened the door and a man was standin there all out of breath. I couldn't understand what he was sayin. He was trying to say sumethin, but he was trying to catch his breath as well. He was sayin sumethin about Josiah being in an accident and gettin hurt at the mill. My heart just dropped. I couldn't think of nuthin but my Josiah being dead. I threw down those sheets and started runnin as fast as my feet would carry me. I got to the steel-mill and my Josiah was lyin there on the floor nearly dead. There was so much blood round him, I couldn't stand it and just started screamin. I knew my Josiah was dead.

I was told one of the belts on the machine broke and knocked his right eye completely out. I just fainted. I couldn't believe what I was hearin. When I came to, I felt a cold rag on my head and somebody tellin me it was gonna be all right. Josiah stayed in the hospital for over a month. I stayed by his side every hour until he got out. I loved that man.

The first month out of the hospital, Josiah wouldn't say a word. I would talk to him, but he wouldn't say anything to me. I didn't know if the man don lost his tongue along with his eye. I didn't know what to do to make Josiah talk.

The more time passed, the longer Josiah stayed to himself. He didn't want to be around anybody. All his friends from the steel-mill kept sendin things over for him. He didn't want any parts of them. The only person he would let come over is Roscoe, and he would talk to him nonstop.

Roscoe and Josiah started workin at the mill at the same time and had been friends every since. Roscoe wasn't married and lived in an old shack down the street. He didn't have any kids. He was always pleasant. He always said yes ma'am and no sir to everybody. Everybody always had sumethin nice to say about him. He was the tallest man I had ever laid eyes on. Every time he came over I would call him, "Long tall Roscoe."

Josiah moods started changin. He stopped makin love to me and stopped tellin me how pretty I was.

When we first got married, every mornin fore he went to work he would tell me how pretty I was, and how happy he was I was his wife. We used to make love like we were teenagers fore all this happened. Josiah stayed in the house most of the time because he didn't want anyone to see him like that. My Josiah was still the most handsomest man to me, one eye and all.

About eight months had passed and Josiah still hadn't gon back to work. His boss said, when he started feelin better, he could come back to his old job and wouldn't have to worry bout a thing. He even started givin us a little money to help us out. I was still takin in as much laundry as I could, but I just couldn't do it all by myself. Lord knows I was gettin tired.

One day I had been workin sunup till sundown washin and takin in white people's laundry. I was comin up the steps into the house with a basket full of clothes. Josiah was sittin on the porch and do you know he didn't even look up or get up to help me carry that basket?

I finally made it up to the top step and looked at him and said, "Josiah, do you think you could get up off your ass and give me a hand with these clothes?"

Josiah started yellin and cursin and fore I knew it, he had jumped up from that chair and slapped me so hard, I went backward off the porch. I went one way and my clothes went the other. All I remembered was hittin the ground.

Josiah was cursin and screamin like a madman. I knew he don lost his damn mind. Not only did my head hurt but also my whole body was achin. I just laid there on the ground tryin to figure out what had just happened. I've been breakin my back all day for this man, and he go and do a thing like that. I didn't know what had gotten into that damn man. He must be crazy hittin on me like that. I shoulda killed him then.

About a week had passed and I had not said one word to Josiah. I would just look at him and he would look at me, and I would look as mean as I could. I wouldn't even let him come into the bedroom at night. I would put a chair up against the door to keep his ass out.

One night when I got into bed, Josiah came to the door, and asked me to forgive him. He said he was ashamed of hittin me and he would never ever hit me again. He said he was goin through a lot and needed to relax. I felt sorry for him and I did miss him lying next to me. All I wanted was my old Josiah back. I knew he was ashamed of his eye, and I had no ideal what he was goin through. He started wearin a patch over his bad eye. I didn't like that patch much because it made him look scary to me especially at night. If it made him act and feel better bout himself, then he could have worn somethin over his whole damn head for all I cared.

As time passed, Josiah got meaner and meaner. I couldn't do nuthin right for him. All he did was complain, complain, and complain. Sometimes when I got up in the mornin and saw the look on his face, I knew what type of day it was gonna be. That was his problem, stayin in the house all day.

He started complainin bout my cookin won't right, my talkin won't right. I just couldn't do nuthin right. Then he started complainin bout me gettin too fat, and lookin old. When he first met me I was big boned and that's what he got when he married me, a big boned woman! Now we've been married all this time and now he wants to complain? Now I'm not good enough for him? Now I'm too fat, and lookin too old? Who did he think he was? He wasn't lookin any younger to me either, huh.

It had been over a year since Josiah was hurt. He ain't got no business acting the way he was actin. Lord knows I have tried my best to make that man happy. I told the good Lord I would stand by my man for better or for worst, and I think he was puttin me through the test.

I remembered another time Josiah started to act the fool.

One mornin I had got up to cook Josiah some breakfast cause the night before, he came into the bedroom and put some lovin on ole Hattie like he was a teenager. I thought somethin had gotten into him the way he was handlin me in that bedroom. Lord knows he could sho nuff make a smile come to ole Hattie's face. I got up that mornin with a big grin on my face and a little skip in my walk. I was gonna fix him one of my best breakfast. I got out my good skillets, and started cookin some fried pork, sausages, grits, and eggs. Now he had treated me right last night and I wanted to do the same thing for him this mornin. I was just cookin and singin when Josiah came to the table and sat down. I looked into his face and could tell that sumethin wasn't right. I was kinda proud of myself for the breakfast I was bout to give this man. I hadn't cooked like this in a long time, but I was glad to have my ole Josiah back.

I sat his plate down on the table in front of him. I looked at him and he had his face all turned up like he smelled shit or sumethin. Would you know, he took one look at me then back at his food, and knocked it off the table onto the floor!

Then all of a sudden he jumped up from his chair and grabbed me by the throat and knocked my head right into the wall!

He started callin me all kinds of names, 'cept for a Child of God. Blood started runnin all down my face. I had the worst headache. I thought when he saw the blood he would stop. After I finished seein stars. I looked right into his one good eye and all I could see was pure meanness, Yeap, just plain ole hatred.

Fore I knew it, I reached around and grabbed that iron skillet I had cooked that fried pork in, and hit Josiah up side the head as hard as I could, and I mean I hit him with all my might. Blood went everywhere. We were two bloody somethin's.

He looked at me with that one eye, dead in my eyes like he couldn't believe, I don knocked the hell out of him.

I yelled, "Yea I got some more of this where that came from," and hit him again!

He looked at me like I was crazy and fell backward into the table and hit the floor. He was lyin there not movin. Blood was just gushin out. I knew I had killed my Josiah. I stared at him for a long time to see if he was gonna move. I leaned down and pushed him in his side and he didn't move. I called out his name and he just laid there. I started shakin him and no movement a t'all. He was just dead.

I started cussin, "Look at what you don made me go and do! Lord, I couldn't help it! He just don pushed me to my limits! He ain't got no business hittin on me like that!"

I ran into the bedroom and started packin as fast as I could. I grabbed my two bags and just started puttin anything in em.

I don killed a man and had to get out of here. "Lord what have I don!"

I found another ole satchel and packed it as fast as I could. I knew the law would come lookin for me. I don killed my husband! I had to leave Louisiana, but I didn't know where to go. I had only one place to go and that was back home to my sister Pearlie's house, and she lived in Topeka, Georgia.

Lord, I don't know why I'm sittin here rememberin all this, but I still remembers it like it was yesterday.

CHAPTER 12

Sophie and I continued dating for the next ten months. She was happy to be with me and I was extremely happy to be with her. We learnt each other needs and want. I wanted to do right by Sophie, so instead of moving in together, I wanted to marry her. I knew we were in love. I wanted to go out and look for a house, but I didn't know the first thing about buying one.

Ms Tiddle Mae became like a second mother to me. I really trusted her, so I decided to ask her to help me look for a nice house. She had become fond of the way Sophie had changed and how she had changed my life for the better.

Sophie was going to church and learning to read and write. I guess she was doing all she could to make me the perfect wife. I was really proud of her.

Ms. Tiddle Mae called me one day and told me she had found the perfect house over on Boykin Avenue. The house had two bedrooms with a big yard in the front and back.

She looked over to me and said, "BoHenry, I want you and Sophie to fill this yards with lots of babies. I've always wanted kids for myself but the good Lord took my husband in the war before I had a chance too. I'll be their grand-mamma."

I looked over the house and thought it was a nice house. I ended up buying it and was going to keep it a surprise until the day Sophie became my wife. I was going to ask her to marry me real soon.

One day, I asked Sophie if she could meet me at the restaurant where we had our first date. She was really happy, because she kept asking me about going back there. As a matter of fact, we end up sitting in the same booth. I was really nervous about asking her to marry me. I didn't know how she felt about me or about being married. We sat down and I talked to her for hours about why I would make her a good husband. She just listened and didn't say much. Then all of a sudden she looked over to me and said, "BoHenry Johnson, are you tryin to ask me to marry you? You ain't got to do all that talking, if that's what you tryin to ask me!"

I held my head down and said, "Yes ma'am, that's exactly what I'm tryin to do. Will you marry me?"

She smiled and got up from the booth, and jumped on top of me and hugged me real tight and said, "Of course I'll marry you!"

We got married on the sixth of September. The wedding was so beautiful. All my gambling buddies from the poolroom were there as well as people from the church Sophie attended. Ms. Tiddle Mae sat on the front row because she said I was her son, and that is where she was supposed to sit.

As far as the honeymoon, we didn't want to go anywhere because neither of us had really been out of Chicago for a long time. I could hardly keep it a secret I had bought a house. I couldn't wait for the wedding to be over, so I could show Sophie how I've been spending my money.

As soon as the wedding was over, I carried Sophie to our new home. She looked at the house and the first thing she said was, "It's perfect."

She just busted out crying, and said, "I can't believe I'm going to finally live in a house I can call my own."

She turned to me and said, "Mrs. Sophie Lavon Johnson is my new name now. I can't wait to show my house to my mama."

I knew my relationship with my mama wasn't good. I had what she had always wanted, a good man. I knew a man had never really loved my mama the way she wanted to be loved. They only loved her enough to keep putting babies up in her. She was still jealous of me after all these years, but I missed her so much. I felt since I was the only girl, we would always be close but I was wrong. I was happy she came to my wedding with all my brothers, but I saw her walk out before the wedding was over. I wanted her to tell me just once she was happy for me, but she left and didn't say a word.

As time passed, Bo started easing off the gambling and started paying more attention to the poolroom. He stilled enjoyed working there but he was even happier with me being his new wife and having a house. He told me he couldn't believe he owned a house and was a married man.

I started going to school to get my diploma, and started working more on the house. I loved that house. Ms. Tiddle Mae started coming around every now and then to check on Bo and me. I over heard her saying she was going to keep an eye on me just in case I backslid. I would always catch her staring at me while she was around us to see how we got along. I thought it was funny.

I talked to Bo about getting a job. He knew I always wanted to have my own money and buy things for the house. I knew he would give me as much money as I needed, but I wanted to work for it. I had to get out of the house every once in a while. I went to one of the department stores downtown to look for work because I heard they needed help. I was willing to do anything to help out my husband. I knew Bo would do whatever I wanted him to do, if it would make me happy. I was finally his wife, and that was all he said he wanted or needed.

CHAPTER 13

After about a year of being married, Bo let me get a job working in The Woolworth Store Cosmetic Department. I was one of the only five blacks that worked there. I knew I could pass for white if I wanted to, because of my good hair and my light complexion. I was very proud of my job and wanted to make sure that everyone I met at that counter knew I was black. I wanted people to be proud of me. I got to know my job pretty well and knew the boss man had his eye on me. Sometimes I would catch him watching me when he thought I wasn't looking.

One day after work, the boss called me in his office to tell me I was a hard worker, and a really beautiful woman. I knew he liked me in a way I didn't want to be liked. He started telling me how well I could do here if I did the right things for him. I thanked him and walked out the office. I always kept my eye on him as well.

When I was behind the counter and I didn't have any customers, I would think of Bo and wished he would find another job besides working in the poolroom. He has been in that poolroom for a long time, and it was a dead end job. I wanted more out of him than that, but he seemed to be happy. I knew he took really good care of me and gave me everything I wanted. It seemed as if I was out growing him. I wasn't as happy with him.

I really did loved Bo, but it was time for him to start thinking about bettering himself. He had never finished school and I figure if I could get some type of education, then he could as well. I thought we both wanted the same things.

I knew after I got this job, he was not going to be too happy about it. I knew he would be thinking about all the men that came through there, but I was his. I still loved him, but something was just missing between the two of us. I knew he was thinking since I had been going to school and to church it was only a matter of time before I started to want something else. I could tell he had started feeling as if he was not the man I wanted him to be, by the way he acted when he was around me. I guess he felt I was leaving him behind, trying to be better than him. But it was not the case at all. I just wanted to do everything I have always wanted to do in my life. I didn't want to have to go back to the life I used to live. People were starting to respect me. I had come a long way since meeting Bo. If it wasn't for him, I don't know where I'll be.

I noticed when we were together; he always got really quiet and didn't have much to say. I didn't know what was wrong with him. He started staying at the poolroom later. I would ask him why he spent so much time there and he said he was trying to give me my space. I told him I didn't need space, just needed him to talk to me.

I knew Bo still loved me with all his heart and couldn't live without me. On some days when I knew Bo was staying late at the poolroom, I would also stay late at work and make a little overtime. I wanted to show Bo I respected him.

As time went on, he still wouldn't talk to me like he use to. He never had much to say. I didn't know what was going on with him. I kept asking him what was wrong, because I knew it was something. He would always just look at me and say, "Nuthin."

I realized after learning to read and write, we really didn't have too much in common. I would talk a lot about books I've read and places I wanted to see. I would look through magazines at different exotic places and asked Bo how he felt about going there. He never had too much to say. I loved Bo and was willing to do anything to make him happy. I just wished he would tell me what was on his mind. Whatever it took to make our marriage work, I was willing to do it.

Once I got that job at Woolworth, and Bo was staying late at the poolroom, Ms Tiddle Mae stopped coming around so much. She knew we were always working and trying to make a go out of our marriage. When she did come around, we had a lot to talk about. I really did like Ms. Tiddle Mae. She was more like the mother I wished I had. I knew she really liked me as well. She was always asking me about when we were going to give her some grandchildren. I would just laugh at her.

One day when she came to visit, and asked, "Where's Bo?"

"Where else besides the poolroom."

"Sophie, can I talk to you for a minute?"

I thought that was strange because she had never asked if she could talk to me before, she would just say what was on her mind and that was that.

She sat me down and started talking about having something to call my own. I didn't understand what she was saying since I had me a house and that was mine.

"You should try to own something that would always bring you in some money. Just in case something happened to Bo. You would be taken care of for the rest of your life. That's exactly what happened to me. I bought that boarding house when my husband left to go to war, and looked what happened to him. Got over there and got himself killed! Girl, you gots to plan!"

She seemed all excited and then she said, "Maybe you should open you a boutique or something. You like clothes, then maybe you should open a place that sells clothes."

I started laughing, knowing that I could never do something like that.

CHAPTER 14

Sophie and I had been married over five years. With time, I thought things would get better between us but it didn't. I felt like I was losing my wife. I thought about sitting her down and talking to her. I knew what I wanted to say because I felt like we were going in opposite directions. I should have told her how I felt a long time ago. I had never liked the fact she was going to school and I couldn't even read or write. Then to top it off she goes out and gets a job at that department store. You would think she was trying to wear the pants in dis here house!

One day when she came home from work, I decided to have a talk with her. I just couldn't keep it in me any longer. When I heard the screen door slammed I yelled out, "Sophie come in here for a minute, we needs to talk!"

Sophie came in and sat down on the sofa and took off her shoes. She leaned her head back and looked over to me and said, "Bo, what is this about?"

I looked at her and she was still the most beautiful woman I have ever laid eyes on. I still loved my Sophie.

I got up from the chair and turned my back toward her and said, "I was walking home today thinking bout our life. We have a good marriage, but I feel you are not satisfied with me anymore. You got an education and a good job and I love you and always will, but something is wrong! You make me feel as if you don't need me anymore."

Sophie looked at me and smiled. When she saw the look on my face, I guess she knew I was serious.

She held her head down and said, "Bo I'm sorry about how I have been treating you. I loved you as well and I loved the lifestyle we are living. When we got married, I thought we wanted the same things. I thought we both wanted to make something out of our lives. Well I have gone to school and got my diploma, now I am working and doing well. I don't know if you want to do anything more than stay at that poolroom. Now don't think I am downing you, but I think you have been there way too long. You are not trying to better yourself. I thought you would go to school or something by now, but you are happy just being where you are. I want more out of you than that. I want us to be able to do things together, go places, and talk about things."

I looked at Sophie to get my thoughts together because I didn't want to say the wrong thing. Listening to her was starting to piss me off.

I turned around and looked Sophie dead in her eyes and said, "Now Sophie, when you first met me, I was working in the poolroom and you didn't complain. The money from that poolroom bought dis here house. I've taken you in and made you what you are today. When I first laid eyes on you, I knew I wanted you to be my wife. You told me all the bad things you had done in your life and I loved you anyway. In spite of it all! Now you think I'm not good enough for you?"

I took a deep breath and said, "Sophie, I am who I am, and I can't be nobody else. I have tried to make you proud of me because I put this here roof over your head and we've always had enough food to eat. I love you! You are my life! I have never wanted anyone else but you. When we got married, you promised me we would be together forever."

I was just talking when I noticed Sophie staring directly at me.

"Bo I'm glad you've finally told me what was on your mind. Why didn't you tell me this earlier? We could have talked about it the same way we are talking about it now."

She looked at me and smiled and said, "All I want is for you to do better than what you're doing. I want good things for the both of us." I got closer and put my arms around her. She moved back. I looked at her and asked, "You don't want me to touch you now?"

I looked her in the eyes and saw a look I had never seen before. I took my arms from around her waist and stepped back. I turned around and grabbed my coat and headed out the door. I looked back at Sophie hoping she would try to stop me, but she didn't.

I started walking towards the poolroom because I knew no one would be there. I needed this time to be alone and think about what was going on with my wife.

I started thinking, "What would I ever do if I lost my Sophie? She was the one and only true person I had ever loved. I could never let Sophie be with another man."

I kept walking and thinking and before I knew it I was at the poolroom. I unlocked the door and looked around. I don't know why I looked around because I knew no one would be there. I went over to one of the chairs and sat down. I just couldn't get it out of my head about what Sophie had said to me and how she didn't want me to touch her. I thought about it long and hard. I put my head in my hands when I noticed a tear starting to fall down my face. I couldn't understand what was happening with our life. The more I thought about it, the more I couldn't help but cry. Sophie was my life.

It had been two weeks since Sophie had told me about how she felt. She knew I was hurting. When we were together, I walked with my head down only speaking to her when I had something to say.

Every time I would look at her, I kept remembering how she looked at me when we had our talk and wouldn't let me touch her. I felt like less of a man when I was around her. Especially when it was time to go to bed.

I decided to start sleeping in the living room. I couldn't sleep in the same bed with her if I wasn't good enough for her. Every night while I lay on the couch, I thought she would come in the living room and ask me back into the bedroom, or even ask why I was out here sleeping on the couch. But she never did.

I knew I was losing my Sophie. I wanted her to ask me back into the bedroom so we could make love. I was missing her so badly. I wanted to feel her, to smell her sweet perfume and look into her beautiful face. I wanted things to be the way they used to be. I wanted to please her, but I could tell she didn't love me the way she used too.

Everything was running through my head. I just didn't know what to do.

I started thinking, "What other job could I get? I didn't have a high school education and couldn't read or write that well. I just didn't feel like trying to go to school again, especially not at this late date. I was doing all right, so I thought. I didn't like school when I was younger and knew I wouldn't do well now. Sophie knew I still made good money working in the poolroom and better money gambling. I just couldn't understand why she wasn't happy with me anymore."

CHAPTER 15

Every morning Sophie would get up to go to work and leave me sleeping on the couch. I wasn't asleep but my eyes were closed. I could hear her getting dressed and fumbling around the house. When she would leave out the door, I would run to the window and watch her walk down the street.

She started to dress more radiant and very professional. I didn't know what to think of this. All I could think about was the fact that it had been over a month since I had made love to my wife, or slept in my own bed. To look at her, she acted like she didn't miss me being in there with her. She never asked me back into the bedroom and didn't have much to say when she was around me. I knew something was going on, I just couldn't put my hands on it.

One afternoon, I decided to walk downtown to Sophie's job. I wanted to surprise her and take her out to lunch. I couldn't take anymore of this. I wanted to talk to her to see what I could do to make our marriage work. Whatever she wanted me to do, I was willing to do it. Even go back and try to get my education. I really missed being with her. I was thinking, maybe after lunch we could talk and work things out and perhaps I could sleep in my own bed tonight. It's been a long time since I had made love to her. Each and every night while I was on the sofa, I could hear her getting up to use the bathroom. I was hoping she was missing me as much as I was missing her. I just knew she was coming to get me off the couch. But it was just only hoping.

When I finally got to the department store, I looked into the window trying to find my wife over at the cosmetic counter. There weren't many people in the store. I finally spotted Sophie and noticed a man standing at the counter talking to her. I looked harder and noticed he was holding her hands in his. She was smiling, a smile I hadn't seen in a long time. It was a smile that belonged to me and to me only.

I continued to stare from outside the window watching the two of them. I stared at him for a long time, trying to figure out what was going on. I thought, maybe I knew him but I had no idea who he was. He was a very handsome man. He was much taller than me, dark complexion, with jet-black curly hair. He was dressed really nice, like he was a businessman or something.

Everything started running through my mind. "Who was this man talking to my wife? How did they know each other? Why was he holding her hands in his?"

I continued to stare into the window when I noticed the man leaning over toward my wife. He kissed her on the cheek, then he started to walk away, but he came back and whispered something into her ear and she started to smile even more.

I still couldn't understand what in the hell was going on. What could he be saying to her to make her smile and giggle like that? Why was he holding her hand? Anytime I try to touch her or say anything to her, she looks at me like I'm crazy.

I was frozen, I couldn't move. Sophie never even looked my way or noticed I was standing there. I watched them the entire time until he left the counter. While walking away he looked back at her and smiled and she waved to him. After he was out of sight, she just stood at the counter with her arms crossed; just rocking and smiling like some little schoolgirl.

I just stood there wondering what in the hell did I just see. After seeing that, I was in no mood to eat. I wanted to find out what was going on with my wife and that man. I got ready to go into the store to get to the bottom of this, when something told me to just go home. Don't start no trouble at her job. I stood at the window not knowing what to do.

I started to walk home. All types of things were running through my head. I thought I knew most of the people she knew, but I guess I was wrong. I was walking, taking my time and just staring out into space. I passed by people who spoke to me and I didn't even say anything back to them. I just wanted to get to the house.

When I finally got there, I didn't even remember walking the distance. It was a hot day outside, but all I could think about was what I saw. "How could she do this to me?"

She would never be able to explain this. I got into the house and sat down on the sofa, and just started crying. I couldn't help myself. "Who was that damn man? Was she having an affair?"

Everything was going through my head. Now I understood why she never asked me back into the bedroom, because she was interested in somebody else. I had cried so much, that I had fallen asleep.

I heard the screen door slam and raised up from the couch. I didn't even know I had fallen asleep. Sophie walked into the living room and just looked at me. She turned her head and didn't even say hello. She walked back into the bedroom and I got off the couch and went back there to talk to her. When I got there, she was taking off her clothes.

I walked in the room and asked, "How was your day Sophie?"

She didn't even turn around to look at me. She just said, "My day went really well, just couldn't wait to get out of these shoes. Been standing on my feet all day and they are killing me."

I just stood there for a moment thinking if I should bring up what I saw today. I just kept standing there not saying a word.

Sophie turned around and asked me, "Why are you standing there staring at me and not saying anything? You got something on your mind?"

When she said that, I got mad. Now I knew why every time I said something to her, she would just go off. After all the things she could say to me. She hadn't even asked me how I was doing, how was my day or even speak to me, nothing! She was acting like I was getting on her nerves or something.

"You know what Sophie, yea I got something on my mind. We might as well get it out in the open. I want to talk to you about two things. First of all, I am tired of you disrespecting me in my own damn house. I ain't gonna keep sleeping out there on that couch no more. If you don't want me in the bed with you, then you go out there and sleep on the couch. Now it's up to you because tonight I am sleeping in my own bed. You make the decision."

Sophie just stood there and looked at me like I was crazy. She didn't move.

"And second of all, I went downtown to the store today to see you early on. I wanted to see if you wanted to have something to eat with me, maybe talk about trying to get our life back together and our marriage on track."

She turned around and looked at me as if she was surprised. I just kept talking, "But when I got there, you were busy. There was this man at your counter. I thought that was kinda strange. You sell lady's perfume and a man was at your counter? Who was that man Sophie?"

Sophie turned toward me and looked me straight in the eyes. I couldn't tell if she was surprised I had caught her or if she was ashamed.

She yelled, "What man BoHenry? There are a lot of men who comes through the store and stop at my counter! They ask questions about the perfumes, what type of perfume to buy their wives, sisters, or girlfriends!"

She continued yelling at me so I started yelling back.

"Sophie you know exactly who I am talking about! The man I saw you talking to, the one who was holding your hand! The one who you were smiling at so freely! He didn't look like he was buying anything to me, 'cept for your time!"

She turned around and looked exactly at me and lowered her voice and said, "Well Bo, if you need to know, he is just a friend. A friend who stops in to see me every once in a while."

Before she could finish her sentence, I cut her off and said,

"What do you mean, need to know? I need to know if a man is tryin to take my wife away from me. Have you told this friend you're a married woman?'

"Bo, I think you are making too much out of this. He knows a lot about us. Yes, he knows that I am married. I also told him we were going through a rough spot, and we were trying to work it out."

I started yelling again, "Damn you Sophie! You have me sleeping out on this couch for the past two months! I can't touch you or barely can say a word to you without you looking at me like I'm crazy! Then I walked down to your job and see this man holding your hand, and you gonna tell me there is nothing going on between you two? Something is going on! I'm not as stupid as you think I am. Go ahead and tell me Sophie, and don't you lie and I mean tell me now! I would hate to have to find him and ask him. Now you better start talking!"

She held her head down and said, "Okay Bo, if you want to know the truth, then I will tell you the truth. When I met you, I fell in love with you. We have been together for a long time and I feel you are in the same place where I first met you. I want more out of life than that and you are not giving it to me. Yea, you took me off the streets and showed me how to be a wife and a lady. You made me happy, and I think I have made you happy. For the last couple of years, I feel we have out grown each other. I have been begging you to do something other than work in that poolroom. We really don't have anything in common. The man you saw at the store is a banker. He is going somewhere and yes, he likes me and yes, he makes me happy. We talk about a lot of different stuff. Things you're never be interested in."

She looked directly at me and said, "And yes Bo, I like him to because he knows how to hold my attention. He's been coming around the store for a while. He's not married and doesn't have any kids. We go out to lunch at least twice a week and yea, I have told him about you. Told him how I thought we would grow old together, but instead we're growing apart. This man makes me feel like we are on the same level. We have a lot of things in common. We talk about far away places and places we would like to go to sometimes. He had been places, but none of that type of stuff interest you at all."

I looked up at her and yelled, "Sophie, you're tellin me you really do like this man? Is this the man you plan on leavin me for?"

"Bo I haven't thought about leaving you, but you haven't got your act together yet. You know what, now that you have mentioned it, I would like to spend more time with him. We like a lot of the same things and I know we could have a future together."

I was shocked, and I could feel my eyes burning and said, "Sophie, what the hell do you mean spend more time together, you're my wife! You can't be spendin time with another man! I just wont allow it! What type of future do you plan on havin with that man? Why are you doin this to me? I have been a good husband to you and I have never wanted anybody else. I promised when I married you, I would love you and be with you till the day you die. You're talkin to me like I'm just some stranger off the street, like I ain't your husband and you ain't got no feelin for me now. You just can't throw me away like I am some type of dishrag."

I sat down in the chair. I couldn't believe what I was hearing.

"Sophie, how long has this been goin on? I know we can make our marriage work. It is sumethin we both have to want."

Sophie turned around and stopped dead in her tracks and said, "Bo, what part did you not hear? I like this man! When he came to the store today, he was asking me about when was I going to leave you? How much more of you was I going to take? He was making me realize our marriage was at a dead end and I was just buying time. What was I waiting for?"

She looked at me and said, "You know and I know Bo, this marriage is not working. It can't and won't work and I'm tired of trying. I have tried to hold on as long as I can."

I couldn't believe Sophie was talking to me like this. She was just upset saying these mean things just to hurt me.

"Please Sophie, I will do whatever I need to do to make this marriage work. Please don't leave me! I can't have a life without you in it!"

I started thinking Sophie had been using me all this time. How could she do this to me? I'm a good man, and a faithful husband. I don't run the streets or chase woman. I can't be any better than that. I thought about everything we had been through since we had been married and felt really bad. I got even closer to her and asked, "Sophie please tell me you are not serious about leavin me."

I could feel a tears coming to my eyes.

"Bo, I am not trying to hurt your feeling, but we both have to face the truth. I think we have ran our course. Yea, I think it would be best if we just moved on. I've been thinking about it for a while now. Just didn't know how to tell you or when to tell you. Now since it is all out in the open, now you know."

Everything started going through my head. I couldn't believe any of this. I got even madder. The next thing I knew, I slapped Sophie in the face as hard as I could. I hit her so hard; she stumbled backward onto the bed. Her whole face had turned red.

She grabbed her face and looked up at me with hatred in her eyes, and started yelling, "How dare you put your hands on me! I hate you BoHenry Johnson! I hate everything about you! Yea, I shoulda left your ass a long time ago. I'm going to get all my shit out of this house and you can kiss my black ass. You can have this house and this ring. Don't you ever put your hands on me again as long as you live and I mean it!"

She started to get off the bed when I jumped on top of her. I was trying to pin her arms under my legs, but she kept fighting me. I grabbed her by the neck with both hands. She was still fighting me. I was little but I knew I was strong. I continued to squeeze and push down on her throat as hard as I could. She started fighting, kicking and trying to get my hands away from her neck.

I don't know what was happening to me because she wasn't pretty to me anymore. I didn't feel the love for her like I used to. I squeezed and held pressure for as long as I could around her neck. I didn't even like the perfume she was wearing.

She was trying to talk, but I didn't want to hear anything she had to say. It was too late. She tried harder to pry my hands from around her neck, but my grip was too tight. She started to kick, but I wasn't going to let go.

I looked into Sophie eyes and I could see her eyes starting to roll back into her head. I pushed down harder until I heard a grunt come from her throat. I couldn't remove my hands. I continued to squeeze even harder until I felt the last of her kick and the last of her grip.

All the hatred I had for her, I was putting it into my grip. She knew I loved her and she was going to tell me something like this? I couldn't let her be with another man. I continued to squeeze until I felt a bone crushed under my hands. I still wasn't letting go.

I continued my grip while I closed my eyes for a minute to clear my head. I looked around the room and then I looked down and saw Sophie for the first time. I didn't know what I was doing on top of her. I didn't even know what happened. I looked around the room again, trying to make some sense out of what I was doing. I jumped off of her and let go of her neck. I watched her for a minute and she didn't move. I spoke her name lightly, "Sophie."

She still didn't move. I said it again louder, "Sophie!"

She just laid there. I started to shake her hard and was telling her to wake up. I looked down at her and the color was gone from her face.

I knew something was wrong, so I yelled, "Sophie, please wake up, I can't live my life without you!"

I started yelling and hollering her name, "Sophie! Sophie! Sophie! Please wake up! Wake up, please!"

I continued to shake her harder, but she still didn't move. She just laid there.

I looked down at her chest and she wasn't breathing, I continued to shake her some more. She was not moving. I couldn't believe I had killed my Sophie, "Lord! What have I don?" I just looked up to the ceiling and started yellin!

CHAPTER 16

I hadn't heard from Josiah and Hattie in a while. I went over to check on em. When I got there, the front door was opened. I pushed the door open some more and called out for Hattie or Josiah.

"Hattie Mae it's me, Long Tall Roscoe! The front door is opened!"

No one answered. I thought it was kinda strange. I pushed the door open some more and stuck my head in and looked around. I didn't see anybody. It didn't look like anyone was home. I went inside and started goin down the hallway lookin in every room and yellin, "Josiah! Hattie Mae! Josiah! Anybody home!"

I got all the way to the back of the house, into the kitchen without seein a soul. I looked down and saw somebody lyin on the floor in a pool of blood. I looked around wonderin what had happened and to see if there was anybody hidin in there. I moved closer to get a better look to see if I could tell who this was on the floor. It was my buddy Josiah. It was a lot of blood all around him and I knew he was dead. I thought about runnin out the house and lettin somebody else find him, but I couldn't do that to my best friend.

I knelt down close to him to see if his chest was goin up and down. I didn't know what to do. I knew nobody could live with all this blood outside his body. I put my hand on his chest for a long time before I felt it rise just a little. I was so happy he wasn't dead.

I ran all the way home and got my car. I put him in and rushed him to the colored folks hospital. While I was drivin, I looked over at him and was thinkin, "That's strange, I didn't see Hattie. Where's Hattie?"

Josiah stayed in a coma for nearly three weeks. I was comin around to check on him at least once or twice a week.

One day while I was sittin in the chair beside his bed, I noticed he had woke up. He was lookin all confused. He looked around the room as if he was trying to remember where he was, how he got there or why.

He looked over to me and asked, "Roscoe, how did I get here in this hospital? What's wrong with me?"

I stood up over him and said with a straight face, "I brought you here. I hadn't heard from you in a while so I went to your house to check up on you. I called out for y'all but no one was home. That's when I found you on the kitchen floor bout dead."

Josiah was still looking confused. He looked over to me and asked, "Where's Hattie?"

I didn't say anything. I was thinking what I was going to say when he asked me again.

"Roscoe, where's Hattie?"

I didn't know what to say, but I thought I should just let him know the truth.

I went over to the window and looked out.

"Josiah, I ain't gonna lie to you, I haven't seen or heard from Hattie. After I bought you here, I went back over to your house to let Hattie know what had happened to you. I stayed there for a while waiting for her to come back home, but she never did. I started to look around the house, and saw some of Hattie's things were gon. It was mostly your stuff in there!"

Josiah got up on his elbows and looked over to me and said, "What do you mean, Hattie's things are gone?"

"Well, just like I said, when I went to tell Hattie I had taken you to the hospital, I didn't see any of her stuff in the house, nuthin at all!"

I turned around and looked at him leaning up on his elbows and said, "Man, you don't remember anything? How did you get your head knocked opened?"

Josiah turned and looked the other way and didn't say anything. Then he looked at me like he was trying to remember something.

All of a sudden he put his head back as far as he could, and yelled! "Damn that Hattie! She don knock my head open and left me here for dead! She didn't even have sense enough to take me to the hospital! Not only do I have one good eye but now I've got the side of my head knocked opened!"

I went over to the side of the bed and looked at him.

"Man you better stop all that yelling! They gonna think you crazy and put you on the crazy ward."

He stopped yelling and felled back off his elbows and laid flat in the bed looking sad. He got real quiet. I looked at him when I notice tears starting to form in his eyes.

He started talking, telling me about how much he loved Hattie and how bad he had treated her, the last couple of months, and how he was ashamed of what he had done.

He looked over to me and said, "I still can't understand why Hattie would try to kill me."

A tear fell down his face and he wiped his eye with the back of his sleeve.

"I just don't understand how she could leave me there on the floor nearly dead? I'm her husband and she goes and do a thing like that?"

Josiah laid back on the bed and closed his eyes. I turned back to the window and stared out. I just stood there because I didn't know what to say to him.

After time passed, Josiah fell in a deep sleep and started snoring. I went over to his bed and look down on him.

I whispered to him, "See you in a couple of days buddy."

Josiah stayed in the hospital over two months and Hattie didn't come and see him once.

When I would come up there, the first thing he would ask me is, "Why Hattie hadn't been to see bout me?"

I didn't know what to tell him. Every time I would ask him how he felt, he would always say he was feeling better.

He looked up at me and said, "Roscoe, I just can't understand it. I don't know why Hattie ain't come up here, something just ain't right I tell ya."

After sitting and talking with him, I knew he couldn't wait to get out of the hospital to see what had happened to Hattie. I didn't know what he planned on doing to her.

I left and came back in about a week. The first thing he asked me as soon as I walked through the door.

"Roscoe, have you seen Hattie?"

I walked over to bed and said, "Josiah, you ain't even let me get my coat off 'fore you start asking me bout Hattie. You ain't even asked me how I'm doin?

He held his head down and said, "I'm sorry buddy. I'm just worried about my Hattie that's all."

I looked at him and he was laying there looking up at the ceiling.

I went over to his bed and said, "Man I ain't seen or heard from Hattie. I've been askin around bout her. Every time I ask somebody, ain't nobody seen or heard from her. It's like she just disappeared off the face of the earth."

Josiah leaned his head back on the bed and looked over to me and said, "Roscoe, I promise you, I'm going to find Hattie. I don't know what she's doing, but I'm going to find out. I'm going to hunt her down like the dog she is. She best to be already dead! Whatever strength I have left in me I'm going to use it to find her, and when I do she is going to wish she was dead. I've been in this hospital for a long time and she hasn't been here not once! She said she loved me. Man, that's my wife, but then she leaves me here for dead? I just don't understand that."

CHAPTER 17

It was a really hot day in the middle of July. The sun was bright, and there was no wind blowing. A_nt Hattie and I were sitting on the back of the porch shelling peas.

I asked, A_nt Hattie, "Do you mind if I go sit under the tree with uncle Bo?"

"Jimmy, my Bo don't want you disturbing him, we ain't got much more shelling to do."

I sat down with my head down and continued shelling peas. When the last was done, I got up and walked toward the tree where uncle Bo was sitting. The closer I got, I could tell he was in deep thoughts about something. He was just staring out into space and didn't even see or hear me coming up. When I sat down beside him he looked over to me.

"Uncle Bo, what got your mind so tied up?"

"I was just thinking about my past, Jimmy. I was married to the prettiest woman God had ever made. She was more beautiful than heaven! Her name was Sophie."

He started going on and on about his life in Chicago and how much he missed the city life and his Sophie. I didn't know much about Uncle's Bo's life. The first time I met him is when he start coming around asking for A_nt Hattie. I didn't even know he had been married.

He looked over to me and said, "Jimmy, I really do miss my Sophie. She was the first woman I had ever loved. I didn't know if I could ever love like that again until I met my Hattie."

I sat there listening. I didn't know if I should ask him any question about her because I know how A_nt Hattie gets when she thinks I'm trying to get in her business.

He got really quiet, so I asked him, "Uncle Bo, whatever happened to your wife? Why are you here and she's not?"

"Well Jimmy, my Sophie's dead. The Lord don took her away from me. I miss her so much. Lord knows I'll love her till the day I die."

I looked over to him and whispered, "Did you know A_nt Hattie had a husband, and he's dead too? I can tell, she misses him too by the way she talks. When we're alone, I just look at A_nt Hattie staring out into space. I guess her mind gets real heavy sometimes like yours. That's why y'all got so much in common, because you both don lost the one and only person you really loved."

Uncle Bo looked over to me and said, "Boy, where you learning all this stuff from? You don't know nuthin bout love, you too young. That's grown folks stuff. Now you leave Hattie be. Don't go meddlin in her business."

"Uncle Bo, you ever think you'll marry A_nt Hattie?"

"Hattie sho would make a good wife and I know she'll take good care of me."

I looked up and saw A_nt Hattie coming toward us.

She got up to the tree and looked down at us sitting there.

"Now what y'all out here talking bout?"

"This Boy was just askin me if I was ever gonna marry you?"

A_nt Hattie looked down at me with those beady little eyes and yelled, "Jimmy, what did I tell you about mindin my business?"

I knew what was next to come so I got up and started running. A_nt Hattie started chasing me. She kept trying to hit me. Now for her to be fat, A_nt Hattie was fast. She grabbed me by the end of my shirt and started hitting me. I was trying to get loose but I couldn't.

Uncle Bo yelled, "Hattie leave that boy be! He ain't did no harm!"

"I told him to stop meddling in my business! I'm going to teach him once and for all to stay out of my business!"

I said all out of breath, "I was just sitting there talking to Uncle Bo."

A_nt Hattie finally let me go. She waved me off and started back up to the house with her hands on her hips. Every now and then she would stop and lean forward and take in a deep breath.

I walked back over to the tree and told Uncle Bo it was getting late and I had to get home. He was still laughing.

He yelled out to me, "She didn't hurt you any, did she?"

"Naw, just tired that's all. A_nt Hattie's big, but she can move. I'm going home now."

CHAPTER 18

After about a year, A_nt Hattie and Bo decided to tie the knot. I didn't understand how or where they were going to live. I didn't know if I was glad when A_nt Hattie moved out or not. Mama and me had gotten used to A_nt Hattie's strangeness and all. She was telling my mom I could come and stay with her anytime I wanted. I was thinking she wasn't strange; you just had to get to know her. I knew things would go back to the way they used to be once she was gone. It would just be mama and me.

One afternoon A_nt Hattie asked me if I could help her move some things out of her room. Now mind you, I had never been into A_nt Hattie's room. I walked inside, and it was the strangest looking place I had ever seen. It had the funniest smell. She had garlic all around the inside of the door. Each window was covered with black plastic with candles all in the middle of the floor. I wondered when I heard her saying those strange funny words that I didn't understand, if it had anything to do with any of this stuff?

I kept standing and looking around until A_nt Hattie scared me when she shouted, "Boy I didn't tell you to come up here and just stand around lookin and doin nuthin, start moving some of this stuff into the truck!"

I stayed in that room all day moving stuff and trust me; A_nt Hattie had some strange stuff. While we were moving, A_nt Hattie called me into one of the rooms and said the strangest thing to me.

"Jimmy, if you ever need me I won't be far away. Now if anybody ever tried to do anything to hurt you, you just let me know and I will take their life away from em. You are my Little Jimmy and don't nobody mess with Hattie Mae's family."

I didn't understand why she was telling me this. After she said that, I looked into her face and for the first time I saw A_nt Hattie was not a strange woman. She was just my A_nt Hattie, and she loved me. I was really going to miss her.

A_nt Hattie and Bo moved on the other side of town. A place everybody referred to as the Bottom. It wasn't really far from where we lived. I could've walked there if I wanted too, but I don't think my mama would ever let me.

Time passed and I didn't see A_nt Hattie for a long time. I really started to miss her, so I started sneaking over there without telling mama. I could tell she liked it when I came around. She was always happy to see me and I was happy to see her.

One day when I was over there, she started telling me she was going to start working after the summer, but for right now she and Bo was doing all right.

She looked at me and said, "It's too hot right now to be tryin to take in white folks laundry. It's too hot to be tryin to do anything for anybody right now!"

I couldn't think of a job she could or would do, because she was just too mean and sassy. I looked at her and started to laugh.

BoHenry was still working at the Junk-Joint. He always left in the evenings and came back home real late at night or early into the morning. Sometimes I would see him walking pass the road headed back home.

I remember A_nt Hattie telling me, "One day I'm going to sneak you in the Juke-Joint Jimmy, and you can see what's going on up in there yourself."

I told A_nt Hattie mama calls that place, the devil's playground.

She said ain't nuthin going on up in there but trouble and devil-meant.

A_nt Hattie started laughing.

"That Pearlie is something else. She talking all that junk and I'm just waitin to catch her up in there one day. She's just too high and mighty for her own good sometimes."

Another day, while I was over to A_nt Hattie's, a lady from down the street came over. A_nt Hattie introduced her as, "Ms. Alice."

Ms. Alice was a beautiful nice looking lady. She wasn't short or tall she was perfect. Her skin was kinda on the light side and she had long pretty hair down her back. She seemed really nice and talked real proper. She was telling me she came down here from New York City, and use to live right here in Topeka. She said she lived here a long time ago and hadn't been too long moved back.

A_nt Hattie started telling me Alice and her had become good friends and how they met at the Juke-Joint. Then all of a sudden, A_nt Hattie looked over to me and said, "Jimmy, gon and get us a cold beer from the kitchen."

When I was leaving out the room I heard A_nt Hattie ask, "Alice, are we going down to the Juke-Joint tonight? I really feel like dancing."

Alice started laughing and said, "Hattie you know you're a mess. Yea, we can go, what time are you talking about?"

A_nt Hattie looked over to the clock on the wall and said "Well, what about um around nine?"

"Then nine it is. Girl, let me go home and find something to wear. I didn't know it was this late. You know I have to look good."

Alice stood up and shook her booty toward A_nt Hattie, and they both started laughing.

A_nt Hattie set her beer on the table and looked up to Alice and said, "Girl, gon and get out of my house, cause I know you gonna be late. I can depend on you for that."

Alice walked out the front door and yelled back, "Hattie girl, this time I ain't gonna be late, and nice meeting you Jimmy!"

I yelled back, "Nice meeting you too Ms. Alice!"

A_nt Hattie sat back down in the chair and started staring at the wall. I looked at her and asked, what was wrong?

"I was just thinking about how good things in my life are going since I moved down here. The more I think about Bo, the less I think about Josiah and leaving him on the floor dead. I really miss him and wished things had ended up differently between us. But I had to do what I had to do."

A_nt Hattie was talking and I had no ideal what she was talking about. She was talking so low I could barely make out what she was saying. Then all of a sudden she said real loud, "Couldn't take any chances, I had to get out of there."

Then she got up and went into the back room.

I stood in the living room and I could hear A_nt Hattie humming while she got dressed.

Then she yelled out, "God is good all the time and, all the time God is good!

I yelled to her, "I'm getting ready to go home, A_nt Hattie."

"Okay, be careful going down that road. "Tell your mama I said she needs to come and see me."

"Okay I'll tell her and I'll be careful."

I heard the screen door slam and yelled, "Alice is that you girl?"

Alice yelled back, "Now you come out from back there now Hattie, you shoulda been dressed."

I came out from the back bedroom all dressed up, and looked over to Alice and said, "Girl, you lookin and smellin good. I can't believe you on time."

She stood up and started modeling her outfit. I strutted around the room and said, Huh, girl you ain't got nuthin on me."

We started to laugh.

We headed out the door walking toward the Juke-Joint. While we were walking, I looked over to Alice and notice she was putting some extra moves in her walk.

I started laughing and Alice looked over to me and said, "Girl, what the hell is wrong with you? Why you looking at me like that?"

"As dark as it is girl, can't nobody see you and that ass-switching walk of yours. You need to save that walk for the Juke-Joint."

"Girl don't be jealous, I'm trying to get us a ride. You better start trying to shake that big ole ass of yours."

"Girl, you haven't seen all this I'm totin'. Mine shakes even when I don't want it too!"

Things got quiet between the two of us until we got to the Juke-Joint. We got to the door and noticed how crowded it was. I looked around and saw BoHenry working behind the bar. I leaned over to Alice and asked, "Do you want to sit at a table or at the bar?"

Alice looking tired said, "Girl, it don't matter to me none, as long as I get off my feet. That walk don wore me out."

We both sat down at the bar, and Bo came over and gave us a beer.

He looked over to me and whispered in my ear, "I'm going to keep my eyes on you the whole night, so you better be good."

"Bo, everybody in here knows you're my man, so stop acting silly."

Alice yelling over the crowd, "Thanks for the beer Bo."

Bo looked over to Alice and said "Alice I don't want any trouble out of you either. I don't wont to have to fight off all these men in here."

"BoHenry, you need only to worry about your wife, I'm single and I'm looking for me a good man tonight. You got anybody lined up?"

We all started to laugh when some man came up to Alice and asked her to dance. They got on the floor and started shaking. I started to laugh because even though I was fat, I could out dance the two of them anytime. I knew I could dance the blues. Bo told me that whenever I came up here, he didn't care if I danced with other men while he was working, as long as I let them know I was his woman.

Alice got off the dance floor and came back to the bar huffing and puffing. She looked over to me and made an ugly face. She was all sweaty, like she had really been dancing.

I looked over to her and said, "Alice, you could never out dance me even if I had one leg."

"I don't see you out there on the dance floor."

Alice sat back down at the bar and Bo gave her another beer.

I stood up looking to see if their was anybody in here I knew. I didn't come up here much, so all the people I did see; I didn't know em that well, but I knew their faces tho.

I had my back turned talking to Bo when another man came up and asked Alice to dance. I turned around to try to get a good look at him but the club was too dark. Also he had his back toward me. It was just something about him that made me feel strange inside. I don't know if it was his voice or what.

I was still talking when I heard Alice say, "Not this time but you come back later handsome."

The man went to the back of the room, where the lighting wasn't that good and sat down. I could feel him staring at us from the back of the room.

I started to stare in his direction, trying to get a good look at him. I thought about going back there just to see who he was, or if this was somebody I knew from a long time ago. Maybe he was just checking Alice out.

Bo looked at me and asked, "Hattie, who are you looking at?"

"The man who asked Alice to dance sounded like somebody I knew. I couldn't get a good look at him, cause he had his back turned."

Bo stared toward the back and said, "You talking bout the man sittin back there by himself? I've seen him in here a couple of times, but he always sit in the back and never talk to anybody. He just sits and drinks and then he leaves. He never bothers anybody. As a matter of fact, Alice is the first person I have seen him talk too."

Alice looked over to Hattie and smiled, "See there girl, I told you I got it going on tonight. Don't be jealous, tonight is my night."

CHAPTER 19

Alice had become a better friend to me than I thought she would. I don't have too many women friends, because I don't like no mess. A woman keeps up too much mess, especially a woman with no man. You always have to worry about em trying to take your man, doing things behind your back, yea being sneaky like. Naw, I don't mess with no messy women. Why is it, when your man is no good, they won't try to take him away from you? Ease you from some of your pains and sufferins. You ain't ever suppose to tell a single woman about problems you're havin with your man. I make sure I don't tell Alice any of my business with Bo. Naw, that ain't nuthin but trouble.

I heard the screen door slam and Bo came into the house.

"Now Hattie, I know you love Little Jimmy, but he can't keep hanging around with Alice and you. That boy needs to be with kids his own age."

"Bo, that's my family, and I will tend to them and you tend to your business! When Jimmy goes back to school, he'll be with his own age. It ain't gonna hurt the boy none to spend time with me. I ain't doing nuthin bad!"

"Okay Hattie, then have it your way, but like I said, that boy ain't got no business hanging around with grown people too much."

One day I walked over to A_nt Hattie's and when I got there, the screen door was opened. I stepped onto the porch and looked inside and saw Ms Alice talking to Uncle Bo.

I started to come in the house or yell to Uncle Bo I was out there, when I heard Ms Alice say, "Bo, I like Hattie and she has become like a sister to me. You know she's not treating you right. If I had a hard workingman like you, I would definitely make sure he was treated right. He wouldn't want for nothing."

Bo just sat there looking at Alice.

"So Alice, let me get this right. You feel Hattie is not treating me right, hum?"

Alice moved closer to Bo and started rubbing up against him.

"Well Bo I could show you how a real man should be treated."

She took her hands and start running it through Uncle Bo's hair.

"Bo do you love Hattie?"

Uncle Bo knocked Alice hand away and got up from the chair.

"Let me tell you something Alice, I love Hattie with all my heart. She makes me happy, and I'm just fine with the way she treats me. We have been through a lot together. That means a lot to me to have a woman to stand by my side."

Alice standing with her hands on her hips.

"Bo, how can you love Hattie? She's fat, and not that nice looking, and she's always talking trash. Look at me. I can get any man I want."

"Well Alice, no you can't get any man you want because I don't want you. I don't appreciate you talking about my wife either. I know your type. I know your type all to well. I was married to your type. She was the prettiest woman in the world and to me she was nuthin but trouble. You are right, you are beautiful I'll give you that, but you are miserable and lonely as well!"

Alice started to walk away but then she turned around and said, "You're the one who's missing out Bo."

"Well, you can't miss what you ain't never had."

Alice turned back around and started walking toward the screen door. When she opened the door she saw me standing on the porch. She got so close to me that I could feel her breathe on my face.

"Jimmy, how long have you been standing out here?"

"Long enough to hear and to know."

She gave me a mean look and said something under her breath and walked down the steps towards her house. I watched her walk away. When she got down the street she turned around and looked back up towards the house.

I turned around and walked inside the house and saw Uncle Bo sitting at the table with his head in his hands.

"Uncle Bo, how you doing?"

"I'm all right, how you doing?"

I started telling him I was standing on the porch and heard everything Ms. Alice was saying about A_nt Hattie.

"Uncle Bo, you know she's not A_nt Hattie's friend. Are you going to tell A_nt Hattie what she was trying to do?"

"Nope, I'm not going to say nuthin and you don't say nuthin either. You hear me! I am going to leave well enough alone. Ain't no need in upsetting Hattie. Just ain't no need."

I looked around the room and said, "Uncle Bo, where is A_nt Hattie, she ain't home?"

"Naw, she's gone to the store. I thought she'd be back by now."

"I know you are not going to let Ms. Alice come over here after all she said bout A_nt Hattie?"

Uncle Bo turned around in his chair and faced me and said, "Now Jimmy, this time Hattie is right. You have to mind your manners, and stay out of grown folk's business. I don't want you to tell Hattie anything that was said today. I will deal with that. Now you understand me?"

I couldn't understand why he didn't want me to tell A_nt Hattie about what Ms. Alice was saying, so I just said, "Yea, I understand. I won't tell A_nt Hattie."

CHAPTER 20

I knew Bo was going to tell Hattie what I've said. If he didn't say anything about it, I knew Jimmy was going to tell her. I realized after seeing Jimmy on the porch, I shouldn't have done what I did. A few days went by and I knew nothing had been said, because Hattie hadn't come over to my house raising hell. Everybody in town knew about Hattie's mean streak and if she heard about what I had done, she would have come over the same day it happened.

I knew the coast was clear and decided to go on over to Hattie's. When I got there, I couldn't tell if anyone was home or not. I kept knocking on the door but no one came to the door. I decided to go around to the back of the house to see if anyone was back there. The window was up in the back bedroom and I could hear Hattie humming.

I yelled up to the window, "Hattie, its me Alice, you going up to the Joint tonight?"

Hattie, looked out the window and yelled, "Well, I don't know. I was thinkin bout it. Might as well since Bo has to work tonight."

She came out on the back porch with some clothes in her hand and looked down at me kinda strange and said, "What you doin round here in the back?"

"I've been knocking on the front door and nobody came, so I went around to the back to see if you were back here."

The sun was shining in my eyes, so I put my hand over my eyes and said, "Girl, you sure you going out tonight? I need to go because I have been without a man for too long. I don't know if I can stand it another night."

Hattie smiled and said, "Alice you know you're sumethin. You going to mess around and get yourself in trouble."

"Well I hope you're not talking about trouble as far as getting a baby, cause girl if I can have a baby, then you better call the undertaker."

We both started laughing.

"What time does Bo go to work tonight, Hattie?"

She held her hand up like she didn't know and said; "I think he usually goes up there around nine, why you ask?"

"I was just wondering if you was going to walk up there with him or if you wanted to walk with me?"

Hattie looked confused and said, "I think I'll just meet you up there since I want to talk to Bo bout sumethin.

I looked around and noticed I hadn't seen or heard Bo.

"Hattie girl, where is Bo?"

"He said he had to go into town to take care of some business, he shouldn't be gone too much longer."

"Well, I guess I'll see you later on tonight; I don't feel like walking up there by myself, but I guess I don't have a choice. Maybe I could try to find me a ride."

Hattie turned and said, "I should be there fore eleven, you sure you gonna be aight?"

I turned leaving from the back yard and said, "Yea, I'll be all right, I'll see you then."

I walked all the way back up to the living room and looked out the window watching Alice head down the road. When Alice got out of site, I started feeling kinda sorry for her. I said out loud, "Alice don't have any real friends but me. Lord what did she do fore she met me? She's runnin in an out of that Juke-Joint tryin to meet a man. Ain't no real good men up there. She needs to go to church, and Lord knows I needs to be sittin right up in there with her."

I started thinkin more about Alice and was wonderin if I knew any good men that I could introduce her to. But all of the men I knew, Alice knew and I think she knew them just a little too well.

CHAPTER 21

Once Bo and I got up to the Juke-Joint, people were already there. Bo went behind the bar and put on his apron. I just sat there at the bar enjoyin myself, listenin to the blues.

Bo came over and asked, "Hattie, you want something to drink?"

I told him a beer.

I sat there listenin to the music and lookin round the club, when I noticed this woman I had seen many times before, kept lookin at me. I didn't know what to think of her. Every time I turned my head, I could still feel her starin at me. I tried not to keep looking back at her, but she kept starin at me, making me feel uncomfortable. I knew a lot of women wanted Bo. I had to stay on my P's and Q's, because I'm not dumb. I knew what was goin on up in here.

I didn't like sittin at the bar with my back turned, so I would always turned around on the bar stool and sit sideways. I had just finished my drink, when I saw this woman comin towards me. I didn't know if she knew me or not. I had been gon along time and maybe she remembers me. I couldn't get a good look at her until she got closer. I knew I had seen her in here a couple of times, but she ain't never looked at me like she looking at me now. She was gettin closer and keepin her eyes fixed on me, so I kept my eyes fixed on her. She was comin right up on me. When she got closer, I noticed she had sumethin in her hand. As soon as she got beside me, I noticed it was a blade. She swung that blade as fast as she could and slit me on my left arm. I fell backward off the bar stool and the woman dived right on top of me. I was wonderin what the hell was goin on, while tryin to keep that crazy woman from cuttin me. I tried to fight her off, but she had that blade and I had to be careful of it. When the woman swung at me again, I put my arm up to block the knife from cuttin me in the face, and it got me on the same arm again. I reached back with all my might and hit the woman in the face and knocked her backward off me. I tried to get up from the floor fore she got back on me. I jumped up and reached in my bra and pulled out my butcher knife.

I looked at her and said, "You damn heffa, what the hell don got into you? What's wrong with you?"

She came charging at me again, and I tried to move out of her way but she stabbed me right in the left side of my chest. I took my knife and just started cuttin. I started waving that knife through the air like I was crazy. All I could feel was the knife goin in and out of this woman. After what seemed like forever, I started to feel hot and my clothes were soakin wet and the room was getting darker and darker. I didn't know what was goin on. All my strength was leavin me. I was feeling weak. I couldn't hold myself up any longer, so I fell to the floor feelin all I needed was to lie down for a spell, maybe rest a minute.

After what seemed like a while, I heard BoHenry callin my name. I could hear his voice and sometimes I couldn't. I tried to say sumethin, but my words wouldn't come out. I didn't know if I was goin in and out of consciousness. I tried to look around to see what was goin on. I looked around and saw the other woman lyin beside me in a pool of blood. I felt weak; all I wanted to do was rest. I faded off while hearin BoHenry and Alice callin my name. They would have to wait cause I was tired and needed to rest.

Everybody in the bar had gathered around Hattie and this woman. Both women were lying on the floor covered in blood. Somebody was asking if they were both dead. I didn't know what to do. It all happened so fast. I didn't even have time to react. Now my Hattie was lying here dying.

I looked over to Alice and said, "Alice, I've got to get Hattie to a hospital."

Alice cried, "Lord Bo, please tell me what just happened?"

"Alice I don't have time for you right now, I have to get Hattie to a hospital! Somebody get a car!"

Alice still crying asked, "Bo, do you want me to ride with you?"

"Lord I just have to get Hattie to a hospital. Please don't let her be dead."

On the way to the hospital, I sat in the backseat of the car holding on to Hattie's hand. I guess I was trying to make some sense out of all this. I kept replaying what had happened in my mind, and all I could remember was Hattie was sitting at the bar stool talking to me. This woman was coming over towards the bar. I didn't see a knife in her hand. I wondered what business she had with Hattie?

I yelled out, "Why did she try to kill my Hattie?"

Alice looked over and touched me on the hand, and said, "Bo, it's going to be all right, Lord knows Hattie's a strong woman. She's in the Lord's hand now. You gonna have to leave it up to him."

CHAPTER 22

I stayed in the hospital for nearly a month. The doctors said my left lung was punctured. I couldn't understand why this woman who I didn't know was trying to kill me. I asked around about her and came to find out her name was SallyJane. Everybody around town was talking about it. I found out some man had paid her to try to kill me. I couldn't understand what in the world was going on, but I had killed the woman in self-defense. She almost got me first, but I got her.

I started askin around to see if I could find out more about this SallyJane and the man who suppose to have paid her to kill me. Every time I asked somebody about it, they acted like they didn't know nuthin. I knew I had to get to the bottom of this or it was gonna kill me. I couldn't just let this happen again and get caught off guard the way I was. Naw, can't let it happen again. It was bout to run me half crazy. I started askin people, even my neighbors, Bertha and JohnLee Tymes if they had seen a strange man or heard about somebody new in town. They said hadn't nobody new been around that they knew of.

Once I started feelin like my ole self, I didn't go back up there to the Juke-Joint for a while. People would be on their way up there and stop and talk to me. I would hear different things about this SallyJane. I wasn't really interested in her; I was only interested in the man who paid her to kill me. I didn't even know if there was such a man or if this mess was made up. I kinda figure it was, cause I knew most of the people who hung out up there. If I didn't know em by name, I knew em by face. This just stayed on my mind real heavy every day.

I remembered seeing SallyJane a couple of times before. She was always nice to me and I knew she liked to flirt with the men in the bar, but mostly she stayed out of the way. Whenever she would see me out in the street, she always spoke. I never knew her name or anything about her.

CHAPTER 23

One hot afternoon, I was sitting on the porch just thinking to myself. I knew my neighbors, Bertha and JohnLee, but I didn't have much to say to them because they stayed to themselves and never came around. I liked quiet neighbors. I wanted to keep it that way. I was looking out in the field when I saw Bertha coming up the road toward the house holding something in her hands. I just sat on the porch watching her get closer and closer. She finally made it up to the house.

Bertha, looking tired and worn looked up to me and said, "Lord it sho is hot. I came to check on Hattie, Bo. I heard bout what happened down there at that place, and I came by to see how she's doin. I want to see if it was anything I could do around the house that needed doin. I cooked some food cause I didn't know if she had been feelin up to it lately."

I always felt it was something strange about Bertha. I just couldn't put my hands on it.

I looked back at Bertha and asked, "Can I get you some water or something?" Cause like you said, it sho is a hot one today."

"Thank you BoHenry, but I'm fine. Don't need no water. That walk ain't that far."

I kept looking out in the fields and said, "Gon on in the house Bertha, Hattie's back there in the bedroom. She hadn't been feeling like herself lately."

Berthas headed up the steps. I started to get up and open the door for her when she looked down at me and said, "You don't have to get up Bo, I can find my way myself. Gon and stay out here on this porch and rest. Lord knows your mind is heavy."

I opened the door and walked inside. I have never been inside their house before and didn't have any idea where I was going. I started walking down this long hallway peeking in each and every room to see where Hattie was. I got to the last room of the house where I noticed Hattie sitting up on the bed with her back towards the door. I couldn't see what Hattie was doing, but she had her head down, rocking back and forth and saying some strange words over and over again. I tried to listen harder, but I couldn't understand what she was saying. Seen like she was speaking in another tongue. Those words seemed like they could've been mighty powerful. She had something in her hand she was squeezing real tight. I couldn't tell what it was, but she wasn't about to let go of it. I didn't know what to do standing there seeing all of this. The faster she talked, the faster she rocked. Then all of a sudden she flung herself backward laying flat on the bed. My eyes almost popped out of my head seeing this. My heart was racing trying to figure out what to do. I took some steps backward down the hall trying to be all-quiet like. Once I got back far enough, I started to call her name like I was just coming into the house. When I approached the door again, Hattie was sitting on the bed all-calm like. She turned around and looked at me.

At first I could tell she didn't know who I was, then I said, "Hattie, I was just coming down here to check on you and see what I could do around the house."

She just stared at me. She blinked her eyes and said, "Bertha is that you? Lord girl! You didn't have to walk all the way down here in this hot sun to check on me!"

I smile and said, "Lord knows I couldn't just sit home knowing what you've been through. I know I don't come around much, but Hattie, I try to mind my own business and stay to myself. I thought if it is anything you need doing around here, then I could do it for ya."

I looked at Hattie and asked, "Have you had the strength to cooked today, have you feed Bo?"

"Naw, I guess it slipped my mind bout cookin. Ain't hungry myself."

"Well Hattie, I bought y'all a big pot of greens and ham hocks. I know it ain't much, but it's what I got. I thought I could come here and help you make a mess of corn bread."

Hattie got up from the bed and came out the room. I stood on her side and held her by the arm to keep her steady. She started walking slowly toward the kitchen. When we got there she looked around the kitchen like it was her first time being in there. She looked over to me and said, "Now Bert, I know I got some corn mill round here somewhere. I just don't know where I put it. Lord my mind is leavin me."

"Now Hattie, you take your time, you just show me where everything is and I'll take care of the rest. Just sit down here at the kitchen table and rest, so we can talk. Ain't no need in rushing. Bo don't look like he's starving any."

I started smilin thinkin about what Bertha said and thought to myself, "Bo was gaining a little weight round the middle, I got to go easy on my cookin."

I started getting things out the cabinet Bertha would need to make the corn bread. I sho was glad Bertha had come over, because I don forgot all about cookin and didn't feel like doin it no way.

I needed to see someone face other than Bo's. It's not that I wasn't glad Bo was here; it's just I needed a little outside company.

Bertha started making the cornbread, and started humming.

I looked over at her and said, "Here baby, put on this here apron. Ain't no need in messing up your good clothes."

I sat there listening to Bertha's humming and thought it was so soothing. I couldn't name the song, but I knew I had heard it before, maybe as a child.

Once Bertha had put the cornbread in the oven, she came over to the table and said, "Hattie, I'm gonna put these greens on and warm them up just a bit. If there's anything else needs doing, just let me know. I don't mind doing it baby."

I looked down at the old tablecloth on the table and said "Bert, I just want to thank you for comin over. The Lord knows your heart and you sho got a good one."

Bertha looked up at me and didn't say anything. Then she said, "Hattie baby, I felt you could use some kind of comforting after what you've been through. Don't worry you're going to be just fine. The Lord will work it out. You just wait you'll see!"

"Bertha, I just don't understand it, why would somebody try to kill me? I ain't been messing with nobody. I remembered when I was a young girl Bert, and my Aunt Mable used to always tell me I should turn over my soul. At that time, I was a youngun and I didn't know what she meant. But I understands her just fine now. I know exactly what she was trying to tell me.

"What in the world does those words mean Hattie Mae, a turning over your soul?"

I looked Bertha straight in the eyes and said, "I take it like this Bert. When you turn over your soul, it's like turning over soil. You tilling the dirt over, where the fresh dirt is on the top, and the old dirt is on the bottom. So with the fresh dirt, you can start over a new life, make amends with yourself, and the old dirt, that's your past, which you have to bury and leave behind."

Hattie threw her head back and said, "Lord knows I'm trying to turn over my soul, but troubles keeps finding me. I just don't understand how this could have happened."

I looked at Hattie. I was still confused and didn't know what to say. But I did know I didn't want any parts of somebody else's problem, and Hattie sounds like she's had a lot of them in her days. I sat there looking around the kitchen, listening, and waiting on the cornbread and greens to be ready.

CHAPTER 24

Bertha and JohnLee Tymes had been living in the Bottom all their life. Everybody in the Bottom was poor. Nobody knew they were poor, because everybody had the same. No more, no less. They all borrowed from each other, and what may have been a good week for one family was a bad week for another. So everybody lived in harmony.

Bertha and JohnLee has a son around the same age as Jimmy. His name is JohnLee Jr. Everybody called him Junior. Junior and Jimmy are best friends. They have been friends every since they were little. They were inseparable they were like brothers.

One day Jimmy came over to my house, and started telling me about what he heard Ms. Alice telling Bo about his A_nt Hattie.

He looked over to me and said, "Junior, this been on my mind every since I heard em talking. I know I have to tell somebody, but Uncle Bo told me not too. What am I gonna do?"

I looked out in space and said, "Well what you want me to do about it? I can't do nuthin. That's grown folk stuff. If it botherin you that much then maybe you should tell my mama."

"Naw Junior, I told you uncle Bo don't want me tellin nobody."

"Do you want me to tell my mama about it?"

Jimmy held his head down and said, "I don't know Junior, I just don't know."

That evening I was sitting on the porch with my mama. I started thinking bout what Jimmy had told me. I started telling my mama everything.

Mama looked over to me and said, "Now Junior, you don't go around repeatin stuff people tells ya. You know better than that."

I looked up at her and said, "I aint told nobody but you. I don't know why Jimmy was telling me anyway!"

I left to go over to Hattie's the next day, and Bo was sitting on the porch again, just rocking back and forth.

I got up on the porch and Bo looked up and put his hands up to his eyes to shield the sun and said, "Bertha, that was mighty kind of what you did yesterday. I 'preciate it from the bottom of my heart. Lord knows if you need anything fixin, just let JohnLee know I'll help him. I won't mind a t'all. Lord knows I won't."

"Ain't do nuthin much Bo, just passing my blessing that's all. Just passing my blessing."

"Well I just want to say thank you again, and by the way, Hattie's back there in the kitchen, so gon and make your way on down the hall."

I opened the screen door and started walking down the hall and found Hattie already in the kitchen. She turned around and smiled. I could tell she was glad to see me. She came over and hugged me and said, "Bertha, I 'preciate what you don for me yesterday. Lord's know I do. I was feelin mighty bad. Come on in here girl and sit down a spell."

I looked Hattie up and down and said, "Hattie, you're looking real good this afternoon. All you needed was a little rest. It's a shame what a little rest will do for ya."

Hattie sat in one of the chairs and look over at me and said, "Bert, how u feelin? You looking as if sumthin is on your mind. You all right?"

I sat down and looked directly at Hattie and said, "Hattie, you know I try to stay to myself, and mind my own business. Your Jimmy told Junior something I think you should know about. Now if I'm gettin out of line, you just tell me to hush-up."

"Bertha, if you got sumethin on your mind, or sumethin to say, now you just say it."

Bertha lean over across the table and said, "It's bout some talking that was heard between Bo and that woman named Alice. Now you know I don't like that Alice much. I don't like her kind. Now I don't know much bout it, and I don't like to spread gossip, but I think you need to ask your Bo what was said."

Hattie got up from the chair and closed her housecoat, looking deep in thought and said, "I knew there was sumethin bout Alice that was bothering me, sumethin I couldn't put my hands on. She was too sumethin, just don't know what it was, too sumethin not right! I know for the last couple of weeks, Alice been actin mighty strange like."

Hattie looked straight at me and said, "Bertha, I'm going to deal with Alice. I don't know if she had sumethin to do with me gettin stabbed or not, but I'm gonna ask her bout what she said to Bo."

Hattie started acting as if she couldn't sit still. I could tell she was getting all worked up, and this was getting the best of her. She would sit down and talk for a minute, then she would stand up, then she would sit back down again and keep talking.

She stood up and looked at me with this strange look on her face.

"Why would Alice be talkin to Bo bout me for? That's my man, not hers. I should march right on over there Bert and get to the bottom of this. That's exactly what I should do, but you know what? It's too soon to be tryin to deal with this right now, but once I start feelin better, she is gonna have to deal with me and I mean it. When I first met her I remember tellin her I didn't like havin a woman with no man round me. Cause it starts too much mess."

Hattie started looking around the kitchen, like she was looking for somebody.

"Is BoHenry still out there on that porch?"

I didn't have a chance to answer before she started yelling, "BoHenry, BoHenry Johnson, come on in dis here house. I want to talk to you bout sumethin!"

Then she turned to me and said, "Bertha now this just makes me mad."

I heard Hattie callin me all the way from the kitchen. I just kept sitting in my chair. She yelled out for me again, but louder. I got up and went into the house taking my time. I knew Hattie was about to talk to me bout something I didn't feel like being bothered with. The closer I got to the kitchen, the slower I started walking.

Once I got to the kitchen, I looked at Bertha, then over to Hattie.

"Hattie, why you calling me from the porch like that? The whole town can hear you hollin. What's wrong with you!"

Bertha looked over at me and got up from the table and said, "Hattie, I think I'll gon on home now. If you need anything else doing, I'll check on you in a couple of days."

Bertha started up the hall and looked back and said, "Bo, you take good care of Hattie cause you knows she's not that well now. Don't let her get herself all worked up bout nuthin."

As soon as Hattie heard the screen door slam and knew Bertha was out the house, she turned to me, "Bo, I heard Alice was over here talkin to you bout sumethin. Now what was that talkin about?"

I knew this day was going to come, because I knew how Jimmy felt about Hattie. I knew Jimmy would find a way to tell her one way or another.

"Hattie, dis ain't no time to be talking about that. You're not that well and ain't no need in trying to get upset over some hearsay. We'll talk about this some other time."

I turned and walked out the kitchen toward the porch waiting for Hattie to call me back. I got to the front door and sat back down on the porch in my rocker and watch the sun start to set.

Hattie stayed behind in the kitchen, and I could hear pots and pans banging. I knew she was mad but I was hoping she would let this go for today. This was not a good time and I didn't want to cause any commotion. All I wanted was for Hattie to heal and be her ole self again. I felt I had straightened Alice out and that would be the end of it. I knew Hattie would not just let it be. I knew the time would come when either she was going to ask Alice about it or she would try to get me to tell her.

I couldn't wait to say something to Jimmy about the commotion he was causing in my house. I knew if I said something to Jimmy and Hattie got wind of it, then Hattie would be mad at me. I just didn't know what to do. I started thinking to myself; "I'll just leave it all alone and let it work itself out."

CHAPTER 25

※

One thing about living in Topeka, Georgia, if there's any gossip about anything it's going to get around town fast. I heard about Hattie getting wind of the conversation I had with Bo. I knew she was upset with me. I remember seeing Hattie in action when she was fighting that woman up at the Juke-Joint, so I knew to stay away from her until things died down. I knew I couldn't keep hiding from her, so I decided I would just have to face her and get it over with. I waited for about two weeks before I made my move to go over to see her.

One evening I waited until after dark to go over to Hattie's. I knew exactly what I was going to say and do. I thought for a minute, "I'd better take my butcher knife with me, just in case things get out of hand. I know I can't fight that big woman; I'll have to stabbed her."

I got my stuff together and walked out the front door and noticed a man standing at the bottom of my steps. He looked up toward me and started walking in my direction.

I backed up when he said, "Hello, I didn't mean to scare you, I was getting ready to come up the steps when I saw you coming out the house."

I looked down at his face and he was a handsome man. I didn't say anything, I just kept looking at him.

Then he repeated again, "Hello Miss, how are you doing?"

I said in a low voice, "I'm doing fine."

He looked me up and down and said, "Miss, you can come on down the steps, I ain't gonna do nuthin to you."

"Well what do you want?"

"I just want you to know I have seen you a couple of times up at the Juke-Joint, and I've always wanted to say something to you. I didn't know if you had a man or not. I had to wait so I could approach you carefully. I didn't want to cause no confusion. My name is Jt."

I started smiling while walking down the steps and said; "My name is Alice, Alice Watson. I'm pleased to meet you.

He held his hand out and I shook it.

"Mr. Jt, what can I do for you?"

"For starters you can tell me you don't have a man."

"Excuse me, I don't know where all this is coming from but no I don't have a man, but that's none of your business."

Jt smiled, and it was a beautiful smile. I also noticed he wasn't wearing a wedding ring either.

"I don't want to seem too forward or nosey, but why are you wearing a patch over your eye?"

"Well that means if I tell you a little about myself, then you'll have to tell me about yourself.

He turned his head looking down the road.

"I had an accident when I was younger, but that's been a long time ago."

He looked at me smiling and said, "I ain't holding you up from doing anything, am I?"

I looked down the road toward Hattie's house and said, "Naw, I was just getting ready to go see a neighbor, but that can wait."

"I was just wondering if I could talk to you for a minute?"

"Now Mister, what is it that you want to talk to me about? I've just met you, I don't know nothing about nobody."

"I figure we could get to know each other a little better. I could tell you more about me and I hope you will tell me just a little about you. Then we'll know something about each other."

This was all happening too fast for me. I didn't even know what to say or do. He seemed to be real nice and I had a good feeling about him.

"Jt, would you like to come and sit on the porch? It's a nice night out and we can sit and talk. I'm not going to invite you in my house because I don't like having strangers in my house. I don't know you that well."

"I don't mind sitting out here if its okay with you. Hopefully I won't be a stranger too long. You can trust me, I ain't gonna bite you. Not yet anyway."

I smiled and said, "Okay let's sit on the porch."

We walked back up on the porch and sat on the swing. He started talking about the times he had seen me at the Juke-Joint with another lady, but never a man. All about what I was wearing and how nice I looked. We spent hours talking on the porch about each other likes and dislikes, and plans we had for the future. A man hadn't spent that much time with me in a long time. At least not without trying to get something for nothing. I liked Jt, because he was listening to everything I was saying. I didn't want this night to come to an end but I knew it had to because it was getting late.

Jt looked over to me and said, "Well Alice, I sho have enjoyed myself talking to such a beautiful woman as you. But it has gotten late into the night, or early into the morning."

"Jt, I have really enjoyed talking to you as well, I don't know where the time has gone."

Jt smiled and said, "Alice you are a very nice and beautiful woman. I'm glad I took a chance on meeting you."

"Thank you Jt."

He looked over at me and said, "Alice I'll like to see you again. Would you like to have dinner with me on Friday?"

My eyes lit up because I was hoping for another chance to see him.

"Yes, I would like that."

He looked at me and said, "Alice, we've had a long conversation and I think I might have told you just a little too much about me too fast. You know I am a very private person. I don't like my business in the streets. I guess what I am trying to say to you is, I don't want anyone to know I was here tonight. We can be good for each other, but this has got to be between us. No gossiping to anyone and I mean not a soul about me. Now can you deal with that?"

I was caught off guard by what he had just said. We've just met and he didn't even know me that well. How is he gonna come up on my porch and try to get to know me and then ask me not to tell anybody about him. This man is crazy.

While he was talking to me the whole time all I could think about was telling Hattie and my friends about him and going to the Juke-Joint with a real man on my arm. Showing everybody I could get a man. Now he was asking me not to tell anybody about him? Who did he think he was?

"Well Jt, that's just strange to me. Wouldn't someone see you coming and going from here? How would you get around that?"

He looked at me confused and said, "Alice, I'll worry about that later. Now what time should I pick you up on Friday?"

"This is happening just a little too fast. You are asking a lot from me and we only just met."

"Well, are you going to let me take you out or not?"

I thought about it and said, "Okay, what about seven on Friday?"

"Aight, seven is fine."

He stood up and started toward the steps and stopped. He turned around and came up close to me and tried to hug me. I thought about pushing him back, because he didn't know me that well. He pressed his body up against mine real tight. I could feel a taste of his stiffness between his legs. I couldn't believe all that belonged to one man! Oh, and it felt so good. I almost told him to come on in this house and spend the night. Lord knows it's been a long time since I've had a man. I was in need of some good lovin.

He turned and went down the steps with a smile on his face. I watched him walk out into the darkness. I kept watching him with a smile on my face until I couldn't see him anymore.

I finally walked back into the house laughing. I had forgotten about going over to Hattie's. I went back into the bedroom and looked at the clock. It was way past three in the morning.

I laid on the bed and said out loud, "Mr. Jt, from what I felt between your legs, you'll never have to worry about me telling a soul about you. I want all of you and that to myself."

It felt good to finally have someone to pay attention to me whom I hadn't already been with. Topeka, Georgia is sho nuff a small town with not one good man left in it. Two dead flies are worth one good man here. I laid there and said to myself, "Lord, please let this be a good man."

That morning when I woke up, I wanted to tell Hattie about my new man. I knew she was still mad at me but I just couldn't keep this news to myself. I started to make my way over to Hattie's and remembered what Jt had told me about keeping him a secret.

After I got on Hattie's porch, I knocked on the screen door. Hattie opened the door and looked out at me.

"Well, look what the cat don drugged in."

Hattie stayed in front of the door blocking it with her body.

"Well can I come in or not?"

She stepped aside and said, "I guess. You may as well, you here now."

I walked straight passed her right into the kitchen, and said "Girl, come on and sit down so we can talk. I've got something to tell you."

Hattie followed me and we both sat at the kitchen table.

"First of all I want to say I'm sorry for not coming over sooner to check on you. I knew you needed some time to heal. I knew you would be trying to fig-ure out what happened up there at the Juke-Joint."

Hattie just sat there staring at me. I knew she was upset.

"So girl, how you been feeling and what you been up too? We've got so much catching up to do. The reason I ain't been over here is because I have met me a new man. I hadn't seen him around here before either. He's from out of town girl and guess what, he's a high roller?"

"Please tell me what kind of man you don met? I ain't seen nobody new around here."

"Hattie I know you don't believe me, but it's true."

"Okay, then tell me bout him. How did you meet, how does he look? Does this man have a name?"

"I tell you what Hattie; we won't talk about him just yet. I won't jinx this until I know it's off the ground. When you see me walking with my new man on my arm, don't say I didn't tell you about him, so don't get jealous. But just in case it doesn't work, I'm not going to get all worked up over something that may or may not be."

I started looking around the room all-quiet like. Hattie wasn't saying anything. She was just looking at me with this crazy look on her face. Then she sat up in her chair and stuck her chest out and said, "Alice I got wind, you were talkin bout me to my husband."

It flashed in my mind I done forgot my butcher knife. Damn! I'm gonna have to find a way to get out of this. I sho can't fight this big woman so I said, "Hattie, what are you talking about? Did Bo tell you I was talking about you?"

Hattie got up, and came over to my side of the table and stood directly in my face and said, "Listen Alice and listen well. I don't like no mess, especially after what I've just been through up there at that Juke-Joint. Bo is my man, my husband. If there's anything he needs and if he can't get it from me, then he doesn't need it. Anything you have to say, then you say it to me if it's about me. Now don't ever let me have to give this talkin to you again. Now if I do, then you ain't gonna get a warnin. I don't play when it comes to my man, and my money. Now do you hear me just fine?"

I was scared of this big woman so I said, "Yea, I hear you just fine."

I thought to myself, Hattie would never catch me off guard like that again. I don't know what I was thinking coming over here without my knife.

"Now if you want to stay my friend, then you better mind your place."

I got up from the table all mad and said, "Well now you've said what you have to say, I think I'd better go home."

I walked out the door and headed straight home. I was mad as hell. I started talking to myself. I knew if I had my butcher knife, it would have been no way I would have let Hattie talk to me like I was some kind of child. Who in the hell does she think she is? Shit, I didn't lie. She is ugly and fat. I know the next time I will be ready for that fat heffa.

I thought about Hattie all week. I just couldn't get her off my mind. The way she spoke and all the threats she made to me. Today was Friday and I'll have to worry about that later. I had something better to worry about, and his name is mister Jt. I had to start getting myself ready. I wanted to look my best. I hadn't been out on a date in a long time. I had to get my hair pressed and wash out my good dress. I started thinking about that hug and the way it felt down below and a big smile came over my face. I caught myself laughing out loud. I put on some blues on my ole record player and started washing my dress out. I went over to the mirror and held that dress up in front of me. I started swaying back and forth to the music with my eyes closed thinking about Jt. I was pretending he was the dress and we were dancing together real close like. The music sounded so good. I opened my eyes and saw myself holding that dress in front of me in that mirror and said, "Child, you don lost your mind. I'm acting like I ain't ever had a man before. Let me hang this dress out and get myself ready."

I asked one of my friends if she could come over and do my hair for me. I was sitting in that chair and that girl seemed like she was taking all day to do my hair. Didn't she know I had some business to take care of?

I thought she would never finish. I had to be careful with my hair because she did do a good job. I went and got the dress off the line and started to iron it. I put my music back on and started humming and singing along. I couldn't help but think about seeing Jt again. I just held my head up and closed my eyes and said, "Thank you Lord. Lord, thank you so much!"

CHAPTER 26

I had started looking out the front window at about six thirty. I had gotten dressed kind of early just in case he was early. I sat in the window to see if I saw any signs of him. I watched his car pull up in front of the house. I looked up at the clock and sho nuff it was seven on the dot. I watched him walk up on the porch and knock on the door. I ran away from the window. I stood at the door until I got ready to open it. I started getting nervous. I opened the door and looked that man up and down and he was looking so good. I had to act cool, because I didn't want to act like I ain't ever been out with a man before. Besides huh, I knew I was looking good too.

Jt looked me up and down and all he could say was, "Damn!"

A big smile came across his face.

"Alice you're looking mighty good to me tonight. If you don't mind, I have this special place I'd like to take you. It's kind of far out of the way but I know you'll like it. Is it okay if we go there?"

I was thinking to myself, "This man could have asked me to go to the moon, and I would have just sat in the front seat with a big grin on my face."

I got a hold of my senses and said, "Jt, wherever you want to go is fine with me."

We walked down the steps towards the car when I noticed Jt looking as if he was sticking his chest out. This made me feel good. I could tell he was proud to be with me, and I was proud to be him. I put a little extra move in my walk as well. I was surprised when he came around to open the car door for me. This man was doing all the right things. I got in the car and we started down the road.

Every thing was so quiet and I was so nervous.

"Jt, you know it's a lot of things I want to know about you. I was hoping we could talk and learn more about each other. The first night on the porch, we talked way into the morning and I really enjoyed that."

"Well, hopefully there could be more nights like that one. I enjoyed it as well. That is why I got you here with me."

I started to laugh like a little schoolgirl.

I lean closer to him and said, "First, I want to know why I haven't seen you around Topeka before? Everybody knows everybody around here. The first time I laid eyes on you is when you were at my doorsteps. Do you have family here or what?"

"Now Alice, I've told you I'm a very private person, but whatever you want to know I will tell you in due time. Don't start asking me too many questions too fast, cause I can only answer one at a time. Like I told you earlier, I don't want anybody else to know my business. I know how women like to gossip."

After he said that, he turned his head back toward the road. He just started talking in a real low voice.

"Well let me start at the beginning. I'm originally from Louisiana, New Orleans. All my family is still there. I have two older sisters who I haven't spoken to in a long time. A couple of years back I was very much in love with this woman. When I first laid eyes on her I knew I wanted to be with her. I wanted to make her my wife. My family did everything they could to try to get me not to marry that woman. I would have done anything to have her. Eventually we got married, but we didn't have any children. We both wanted children. A lot of things started happening early in the marriage. We started growing apart. She got tired of me and I got tired of her. I guess she couldn't take it anymore. One day she just up and left me, and I haven't seen or heard from her since. She was a good woman and I still misses her a lot.

I sat back in the seat hanging on to every word. Then he got quiet, and looked as if he was in deep thought about something. I touched him on his hand.

"Jt, I know I asked you earlier about your eye. Exactly what happened?"

"Now about my eye, I was working in a mill and the machine belt broke and knocked my eye out. I have been wearing this patch every since. I remembered the day like it was yesterday. I know it seemed like I've had a lot of troubles in my days, but it's not the case. I've had a good life. I used to have some family here in Topeka but I think they moved away. I haven't been able to find them. I used to stay with my aunt here when I was young, but it's been a long time ago."

"Well who's your family maybe I can help you find them? What's their last name?"

Jt smiled and said, "Naw, I'm going to let it go. I'll run into em somewhere."

"You sure you don't want me to help you? I got good connections around here."

"Yea, I bet you do."

We both started to laugh.

Jt was keeping his eyes on the road. He turned to me and smiled.

"Alice, it's your turn to tell me about you. Why is such a beautiful woman living here in this little lost town? Now that's something I don't understand."

I turned and started thinking not really knowing why I came back. I turned and just stared out the window and started talking.

"Well mine is not a long story. I'm originally from here, born and raised. My mama and daddy are from here. When I got older, I met a good man and he asked to marry me. He loved me and I loved him. We didn't have any children either, but he loved them and wanted lots of them."

I looked over to Jt to see if he was still listening to me. It seemed like he was, so I kept on talking.

"My man was a heavy gambler. I always told him gambling was going to be the death of him and that's exactly what happened. Now I know you ain't gonna believe this, but a woman ended up killing him. Now I didn't know much about this woman, but I heard she was mean. Heard she had the devil in her. She just slit his throat over some money he supposed to have owed her. Everybody in town was talking about it. It just got to be too much for me, to be living here and knowing somebody had killed my husband. Now I don't know much about what happened, but I do know he's dead. I really don't know what was going on between my husband and that women, 'cept that she killed him, and that's something I'll never forget."

Jt looked over to me and said, "Well did you know the woman who killed your husband?"

"Now Jt, you're not even listening to me. I just told you I didn't know this woman. I just knew what people were telling me about her. All I got was her name. Now remember, we're talking about a long time ago. Right after that incident, I heard the woman left town never to come back again. Since it was nothing left for me here, I decided to get away and try the big city. I had always wanted to move, so that gave me my chance. I moved to New York, and stayed there for years. Then I got tired of that and now I'm back. A lot of my family still lives here in Georgia, but not in Topeka. Topeka is a little boring, and it's slowed me down a lot."

"I'm glad you moved back here and slowed down, because then I would never have met you."

I turned around and gave Jt a kiss on the cheek.

"That was really sweet of you to say."

"I just want you to know I'm a serious man Alice, and I hope you're serious bout me."

He turned his head back toward the road.

"The place we are going too is right here on the right."

Once we stopped, I didn't know whether to open the door or if he was going to do it. I just sat there and sho nuff, he opened my door. That made me know right then and there, that this was a good man. We started to walk toward the restaurant and you know what that man went and done? He ran ahead and was holding the door open for me. Lord, can you believe that?

I walked inside and looked around. The restaurant was really nice. We sat down at the table, and Jt asked me what I was drinking?

"I'll start off with a glass of water because anything stronger than that will go straight to my head." I started laughing.

"Well, if that's the case, then you better have a soda."

We both started laughing.

The waiter came around with the menu and asked if we were ready to order. We both ordered pork chop, yams, and collard greens. The food was so good. I was looking around to see if I saw anyone I knew. I wanted them to see me out with my new man, but I didn't see a soul.

CHAPTER 27

Jt and I had been dating for six months, and I was in love with him. I hadn't breathed a word to anybody about our relationship. Jt wanted us to live together but he didn't want to move into my place. He wanted to move out into the country. I wanted to move as far away from everyone if it meant I could have Jt all to myself.

After talking to Jt about our plans, I decided to rent out my house and moved in with him. I knew I was falling in love with him and wanted him to ask me to marry him.

I had never mentioned Hattie's name around Jt, but he slowly started asking me questions about her. I didn't even know he knew Hattie. He even asked me three times in one day, "How long has Hattie been living here? How long has she been married to BoHenry? Where was BoHenry from?" I didn't know where all these questions were coming from. There was really nothing to say since I didn't deal with Hattie anymore.

Since that day she had talked to me like I was a damn child, I haven't had any use for her. I had plans for Hattie. Whenever Jt would ask me something about Hattie, I would just say, I don't know much about Hattie or her business.

Jt started working on the other side of town. He told me it's the man's job to provide for the woman and he didn't want me to work at all. I had my own little money coming in since I was renting my house. So I was all right with not working.

I had never met a man as private as Jt. What or whom he was hiding from, I didn't know. Most of the places we went were out of town. No one came out to visit us, and we never went to visit anybody. We didn't even go up to the Juke-Joint together.

Lord this man coulda killed me and wouldn't a soul know who did it. But you know what? This was my man and I loved him.

One day Jt had just come in from work. I wanted to talk to him about something that was bothering me.

After we ate dinner, I looked over to him and said, "Jt I'm getting bored being out here all by myself doing nothing all day. I feel like I'm just wasting away."

He got up from the kitchen table and came over and put his arms around me. "Now Alice baby, you're not by yourself you've got me. That's all we need is each other."

"Yea, I know I got you but it's scary out here at night when you ain't here. You stay gone all the time. I don't like being by myself. I don't go anywhere and don't nobody come here either. I just don't like being out here by myself."

"Well baby what you scared of, ain't nuthin out here but us? Ain't nuthin gonna get you."

"That's the problem, ain't nobody out here but us."

"Okay baby, then I'm going to have to buy you some company, some protection so you won't be scared."

I thought to myself about what Jt had said and yelled out, "Jt, what kind of protection are you talking about? I know you ain't talking about putting a gun up in this house?"

I got up from the table and started to walk toward the bedroom because I couldn't believe this man was talking about buying a gun.

He followed behind me and said, "Baby, you need to learn how to use one to protect yourself. It ain't hard to learn."

I stopped in my tracks and turned around.

"Jt, I don't know if I can do this. I don't like guns, never have and never will. This is something I'll have to think about. I just don't like guns. Can you give me some time to think about it?"

Jt grabbed me by the hand and said, "Now baby, time is one thing we don't have. Now you know people can get crazy. I'm going to do this now and everything is going to be all right, just wait you'll see. You'll feel better knowing you got some protection."

"Well, Jt, I don't know about this, I just don't know."

Sho nuff when Jt got paid on Friday, he came home with a shotgun. When he showed the gun to me, I backed up like it was a snake.

He noticed the look on my face and said, "Now Alice, ain't nuthin to be afraid of. It ain't gonna bite you. Whenever I get some time off, I'm gonna show you how to use it and how to load it. Ain't no need in having it, if you can't use it. We are out here by ourselves. If something happens, the law ain't ever going to come out here to protect us, so we have to protect ourselves."

I started thinking, "When I told this man I needed company, I meant people company; not the company of a gun. What have I done got myself into? I stared at the gun and then looked back up to Jt.

"Jt, this is just crazy, we don't need a gun! I need the company of people, not this craziness!"

I went back into the kitchen and started cleaning up. Jt went back into the living room. I thought about this gun thing again and again and walked into the living room. He was sitting in the chair with his eyes closed. He looked like he was in deep thought about something.

I asked him, "Jt, have you been to the Juke-Joint lately?"

He opened his eyes and looked at me and said, "Yea, I passed by there and stuck my head in. Why?"

"I was just wondering if BoHenry was still working there?"

"Yea, he's still there and guess what? Hattie was there too."

I was caught off guard when he said that.

"I can't believe Hattie is back up there after what happened to her. I know if that was me, you'll never have to worry about my feet stepping on the inside of that place ever again. I've got to give it to Hattie, she's one tough bird."

Jt started laughing and said, "Yea, I think Hattie has nine lives. I don't know who she prays to but I know they are watching over her."

I held my head down trying to look sad and said, "Well I was just thinking, it's boring out here. Ain't nobody around. Nobody ever comes to visit us. People don't even know if I'm living or dead. It's just you and me."

He got up from the chair and put his hands on my face and said, "Alice don't try to give me a sad look. When we came out here, you didn't want a soul to know where you were going. Now you don got used to me, and now you're bored. You ain't got nuthin to do. You don't want it to be just you and me anymore? You getting tired of me now?"

"Naw silly, we just don't see anybody anymore. That's all I'm saying. You know at one time Hattie was my best friend, and my only friend, but you keep me so locked away. Nobody even knows I've got a man. I do wish we could go out somewhere around here, where we can see people we know."

Jt looked as if he was thinking and said, "I'm going to start taking you anywhere you want to go real soon. That I promise you."

I looked over to Jt, because the way he looked when he said that was as if he was planning something big.

I started thinking about putting my plan to work. I wanted to let Hattie know I was alive and doing well. I knew she was going to faint knowing I was right here under her nose. I didn't know if I could trust Alice with my plan just yet. I loved her and knew I was in this relationship for the wrong reason. I was hoping everything would be over real soon. I wanted my revenge. All this time had passed, and all I had accomplished was my relationship with Alice. I was hoping to keep from hurting her, but what could I do? I didn't know I was going to fall in love with her. It wasn't part of my plan.

CHAPTER 28

꧁

My name is Hattie Mae Wilson. I am the oldest child to George Harold and Katie Wilson. I was born fightin, fightin for life, fightin for air, just fightin to survive. I have been fightin all my life and haven't let up an inch in all the years. I have always felt left out. I couldn't fit in anywhere. When I was younger, none of the girls in school liked me. All they did was talk about me behind my back. They were always sayin things like, "You're ugly, you're blue black with nappy hair, you look and act like a boy."

Growing up wasn't easy. It was hard to make friends. No one wanted to be my friend. None of the girls wanted to play with me, so I started playin with boys. The girls were always sayin I was too rough. Sumetimes I knew I was even too rough for the boys, because I was built tough. Whenever we played sports, they knew whomever team ole Hattie was on, it was gonna be the winning team. I wasn't feminine in no way. I even had a hard walk. My mother was always sayin, "Hattie Mae, one day I sho hope you grow out of all that nonsense and start being womanly. Girl, you're too hard."

I loved my mama and daddy, but I was just plain different. They just didn't understand me. Daddy didn't care what I did, as long as I didn't disturb him. I was never a daddy's girl. Sometimes he would take me to work the fields with him, but only because mama told him to. I didn't mind goin because all the boys I played with were there.

One day I found out my mama was gonna have a baby. I was so happy! I would finally have someone who could love me just for me. I thought we were gonna look just alike since we were kin. Everybody kept telling my mama it was gonna be a girl because of the way she was carryin it. I couldn't wait to have a little sister. It seemed like it was takin mama years to have that baby.

One afternoon, I was comin in from school and came home to find out that mama had a little girl. She named the baby Pearlie Jean. When Pearlie Jean was born she looked nuthin like me. She was nearly white with straight hair. I just couldn't understand it. How could she have looked so different? I hated Pearlie and wished she was never born. I wanted things to be back to the way they use to be. Everybody thought Pearlie Jean was a beautiful baby. No one has ever told me I was pretty or beautiful, even as a teenager. I became meaner and meaner because nobody would pay any attention to me. I knew I was hurtin mama and daddy. I hated Pearlie Jean and knew I could never love her, but the baby started liking me. She always wanted me around her, and would smile and laugh when I picked her up and played with her. She would start cryin when I stopped. She wasn't afraid of me. Nobody else wanted to be around me, because everybody else was scared of me. But I always had my Pearlie Jean to go back home to.

I remember one of the boys in school kept tryin to be my friend. No one wanted to be around him, because he was really odd. People were scared of him, but not me. I wasn't scared of anybody. At first I didn't like him, but with time we became good friends. His name was Lonnie. Lonnie was really tall and skinny. He wore really thick glasses and had bumps all over his face. He was really smart with his lesson tho, but he was just odd. Lonnie was the youngest of three boys. His brothers taught him how to gamble and boy could he gamble. The only time any of the other boys wanted to hang around Lonnie is when he was gamblin.

Eventually he taught me just for fun. With good practice, I started playin with people my own age and I was gettin good at it. I got bored playin for fun, so I wanted to play with the older people for money. Lonnie kept tellin me I shouldn't be gambling for money. That was grown folks business, but being too young to get a job, what else could I do? I would take a little money out of mama's purse while she was sleepin, or just when she wasn't watchin. But after I won, I would put all the money back, and even a little more. I think mama knew what I was doin. She didn't like it, but I could tell she enjoyed havin the extra money. She never told daddy or said anything to me about it, but I knew he had heard about it from the streets, I was gamblin for money.

Daddy used to say, "Hattie Mae, those streets are gonna be the death of you yet. You're a young woman. You ain't got no business doin what you're doin. We didn't raise you like that."

After a while, gamblin became like second nature to me. It made me feel worth sumethin. I was really getting good at it. That was the only time in my life I felt people liked me for me. They would gather around and watched me gamble. Since Lonnie and I had become best friends, I told him, if anybody ever touched or teased him again, they would have to deal with me. Words spread all over the entire school not to mess with Lonnie.

One Friday night I had stayed up gamblin the entire night. It was no school the next day, so I didn't care how long I gambled. Mama and daddy were sleepin, so I would just sneak in the house after I finished. Luck was runnin my way and I was takin everybody's money. Only one man was still sittin at the table and he did not want to give up. He was a real mean man and thought he was tough, but he didn't know he was dealin with ole Hattie. I was tougher. I had taken everything the man had owned, and was startin to feel sorry for him. Once it was all over, he couldn't believe a girl had beaten him. He stood up and looked around the room and started smilin. He looked over to me and said out loud, "I'm not giving an ugly, fat, nasty girl like you another damn thing. If you get anything from me, then you'll have to take it."

Everybody around the table backed up because they knew it was gonna be trouble. Most of the people in there knew me. They knew I didn't take no mess. I stood up and looked the man dead in his eyes. I couldn't believe this man was actin like this after I had beaten him fair and square. I grabbed the man by his collar and pulled him toward me. I reached under my shirt and pulled out my knife and slit the man right across the throat as fast as I could. The man didn't even know he had been cut. You should have seen the look on his face. I let go of his collar and pushed him back off me. He just stared at me.

"You said, if I get anything from you, then I'll have to take it, so that's exactly what I am doin."

He didn't say a word. He looked down at the front of his shirt and saw it covered in blood. He put his hand on his shirt to see where the blood was comin from. He looked back up at me and fell to the floor. Blood was every-where.

That was the first time I had ever killed anybody. It felt like nuthin to me. I didn't feel anything. I looked around the room, and everybody was staring at me. They looked as if they couldn't believe what I had done. I looked around the room at everybody and said out loud, "I will never let a man, woman, or child, disrespect me and I mean it, never!"

I bent down and took everything out of the man's pocket I thought he owed me. Then I decided I might as well take the rest because he won't be needin it where he's goin. I took every cent he had. I looked around the room again and stood up and walked right out the front door without lookin back. I started thinkin bout what had just happened. I didn't know anything bout that man, 'cept he was married. I didn't even know his name. I guessed that killin is what got me my reputation. When people spoke of me round town, they would say, "You know Hattie, that mean, fat, ugly woman that killed that man over some cards."

Daddy had gotten wind of what I had don fore I had gotten back to the house. They were talkin when I walked into the house and told me to come there. I walked into the room and they told me I was getting out of control. They said they had talked it over and decided to send me to Baton Rouge to live with my Aunt Mable. Aunt Mable is my daddy's sister. They said they had talked to Aunt Mable and she said it was fine. I could come stay with her. I remembered her from when I was little. After they finished talkin to me, mama told me to go to my room and pack my stuff, because I was leavin that day.

They put me on a bus and I stood there not wantin to go. What was I gonna do about not seein Pearlie and my friends? I looked at mama and daddy and told them, I promised I would be good. I yelled out loud, "Daddy, please don't make me go!"

Daddy said that it was too late because they heard about what I had done and the law would soon be coming for me. I knew daddy was right. I kissed Pearlie and mama and got on the bus. I waved again at Pearlie. I looked back behind daddy and I saw Lonnie. I wanted to run off the bus to tell Lonnie goodbye, but the driver had closed the door. I waved at him, Pearlie, mama and daddy until I couldn't see them anymore. Mama told me that Aunt Mable would be there on the other end when I got off the bus. She said for me to listen to the driver and he would tell me when I was in Baton Rouge. I cried the entire time because I knew I would probably never see my family again.

The bus finally pulled into Baton Rouge, and I got off. I didn't see Aunt Mable. I couldn't remember how she looked. I hadn't seen her since I was a child. I was standin around when this woman walked up to me and ask me if I was Hattie Mae. I smiled and said, "Yeap, that's me."

She looked me up and down and made a frown. I looked back at her and she was a beautiful lady. She was tall and really thin with white hair. She had the prettiest green eyes. I had never known anybody with green eyes before. She was really pretty and strange to me all at the same time. Aunt Mable has always acted and talked strange to me even growin up as a child. She looked over to me and told me to pick up my bags because we have to walk. She said she was too old to drive. I looked over at her again and said to myself, "Lord what am I in for?"

As soon as we got to the house, Aunt Mable started tellin me the rules about livin with her. She showed me my room. I was lookin over the room, when Aunt Mable looked over to me and said, "Girl I know about you killin. You a child girl, and you should be turning over your soul before it's too late."

I had no idea what turnin over a soul or soil meant, but I know I didn't come all this way to be workin in no garden. I believe Aunt Mable don started talkin out her head already.

For some reason, she started telling me she was gonna teach me how to protect myself. Now she knew I knew how to protect myself because I don killed a man before, so what more could she teach me?

She looked over at me and said, "Just because you think you can go around killing, you think that's taking care of yourself? Naw, that ain't nuthin, protecting yourself ain't the same thing as knowing how to kill somebody. Anybody can kill, but everybody don't know how to protect themselves. You just listen to me. Your Aunt Mable knows some stuff. You are young girl, you don't know like Mable knows. I am gonna teach you some powerful stuff, and I never want you to forget what I teach you."

I was thinking to myself, "This old woman can't teach me nuthin. I'm a young girl, I could teach her a thing or two."

I had no idea what Aunt Mable was talkin bout because I knew she was strange. She was always sneakin and lookin around everywhere as if she was expecting sumethin to happen, like somebody was gonna sneak up behind her. She always acted like she knew sumethin nobody else did.

As time went on, Aunt Mable was really nice to me. I guess she enjoyed havin me around. I was startin to like her as well, but I was missin home. She started teachin me sumethin about some stuff called Roots. I had no idea what this Root stuff was about. She said she was gonna take me to her special place and try to teach me the difference in the roots. Which root did what, what color to pick to do what with. She explained to me I needed to know how to work the roots. Having the root and not knowin how to work it, gives you no power. You have to believe in the power of the roots. Trust me, I had no idea about what this woman was talkin bout.

Everyday doin the summer 'cept on Sundays, she was teachin me bout those roots. I knew she liked teachin me cause I was listenin to her every word.

One afternoon while we were sittin on the porch, Aunt Mable asked me if I wanted to hear a funny story. She started tellin me about her husband, Uncle John. She looked over to me and said, "Girl, do you remember your Uncle John?"

I had to think really hard because I hadn't seen or heard anybody speak of him in a long time. I had forgotten all about him.

She started tellin me about how much she was in love with Uncle John. Then she just stared out into space and started talkin, "John was the only man I had ever loved in my entire life. Whatever it took to make him happy I did. I was willing to lay down my life for him. But over the years, John started changing. He wasn't taking care of home like he used to. The passion started dying out of his love. He never wanted to go anywhere or do anything with me anymore. I thought it was because he was working hard trying to provide for the family but girl, that wasn't hardly the truth. John was working hard all right, working with another woman!"

When Aunt Mable said that, I sat up in the chair and really started to listen. I knew this was gonna be really good. She was still starin out into space and still talkin. "John tried to be slick, but your Aunt Mable was slicker. I started keeping my eyes and ears opened. I heard people talking about John and his other woman."

Then she looked over to me and said, "That's how I found out about her, you know?"

She sat back and started to stare out into space and started talkin from where she left off.

"I didn't know this other woman you see, but I heard she lived on the other side of town. I heard she was really a nice looking woman. She was much younger than me. How ole John thought he could get or keep a younger woman, I don't know. Don't nobody want his ole behind. I didn't know if she knew John was married or not, because you know how men like to lie. But I did know what I was gonna do to ole John. John was my problem, not hers. See I wasn't gonna mess with this woman, because I didn't know what lie's John had been feeding her. I know she didn't do anything to me, so I had no problems with her. My problem was with John."

First of all, I had to play it easy like. Play like I was still the same ole Mable. Like I didn't know bout nuthin that was going on. Couldn't let nobody know what I was doing."

Aunt Mable looked over to me and said, "Now I'm gonna show you how powerful my roots are. You know what? As time passed, ole John started acting really strange."

Aunt Mable leaned over and whispered, "Now Hattie Mae, I'm gonna tell you something and you never repeat it."

I leaned in closer to hear what Aunt Mable was about to tell me. She turned and looked me in the face and said, "I had to work my roots on John. I had to use my strong good roots, fresh picked, right from the ground.

First of all, John started complaining he was feeling tired all the time. Shoot, I felt if he was coming home to me tired after being with his other woman. I thought I'd send him right back to her the same way."

I started to laugh because this story was really funny. I looked over to her and she was still staring out into space.

"I was working my best root on ole John, one that was taking all his strength away. Then after that, John started talking nonsense, talking crazy like. At first it was to himself, then the more I worked my roots on him, the more he just started talking crazy out loud.

You know what? One day John ran all the way from his other woman's house back to here, butt naked. Running and screaming all this crazy talk. The law picked John up right down the street from here and took him to the crazy house. He's been there every since."

A big smile came over Aunt Mable's face.

"Everybody in town don saw ole John's private parts, heh, heh! Running down the street all butt naked! Lord, I would have given my life to see that. He still ain't in his right mind today. He's still up there talking crazy talk. Telling those people at the hospital, I don work roots on him. Now you know those white people don't believe in that kinda stuff."

I looked over to Aunt Mable because none of this was funny to me anymore. I didn't know what to say because I really didn't believe all this root stuff. But after hearing that, I started believing in those roots.

"Hattie Mae, if you stay with me long enough, we gonna go and visit ole John. He won't know who we are cause his mind is gone. He don't even remember me and I'm his own wife."

She looked out into the sun and said, "I betcha that'll teach him to mess around on ole Mable."

I stayed with Aunt Mable for a lot of years. I learnt everything about workin roots. Stayin with Aunt Mable took all of my meanest away. We only had each other. I started to share things with her. Tell her things I had never told anybody ever in my life. About how I kept my feelins locked away and the way people treated me. She said she could understand why I acted the way I did. When she said that it made me feel better. I felt I could talk to Aunt Mable because she never called me names, like fat, lazy, or ugly. I knew I could tell her anything without feelin ashamed. She became my best friend. I wanted to change my ways because I didn't like being mean, evil or nasty.

Aunt Mable looked over to me and said, "I'm gonna show you how to turn over your soul girl."

She started teaching me bout how to walk, talk and act like a woman.

She said, "Ain't no man gonna want a woman who can throw an axe better than he can. A man wants a woman who acts like a woman."

I started laughing because Aunt Mable sho do say some of the funniest things.

I started thinking bout my life in Topeka, and the things I had don. I knew I had don a lot of bad things, all that killin and all. I had to let that part of my life go. I missed being home but I knew I couldn't go back till things cooled down.

Mama, Daddy, and Pearlie Jean came down to Baton Rouge to see bout me every chance they got. Pearlie was always happy to see me. She was really growin up fast. Mama and Daddy was happy to see the changes bout me that Aunt Mable kept tellin them that she was responsible for. When she said that, it always made me laugh.

Well, I guess if it wasn't for Aunt Mable, I'll still be the same ole Hattie.

I knew it would be a long time before I ever went back to Topeka. I was really gonna miss them, because they were all I had in my life.

CHAPTER 29

❀

Hattie was sitting on the porch when I came outside. I looked down at her and said, "I think I'll go up to the Juke-Joint early today. I want to make sure the place was cleaned up pretty good last night and to see what needs doing fore it's time to open. I won't be up there too long Hattie Mae."

I started walking towards the Juke-Joint and when I got there a young man was sitting on the steps. It wasn't anyone I had seen before. I walked up towards him and said, "You kind of early ain't you partner?"

The young man looked up at me and said, "I ain't here to do no drinking mister."

I looked down at him and ask, "Then why you sitting here in this hot sun for?"

The young man stood up and looked me directly in the face as if he was trying to get a good look at me.

"I'm looking for work, any kind of work. I heard you might have some work here. You the man who runs this here place? I thought maybe I could do something in there that needs doing. I'm a good worker and I work really hard. I need to make some money."

"I've never seen you here at the Juke-Joint before, are you from around here?"

"Naw, I'm a traveling man. Planning on making my roots right here. I don't know how I stumble on this little town, but I think I like it here. Wouldn't mind making it my home."

I was listening to the way he talked, because I could tell he wasn't from around these parts.

"What's your name boy?"

"My name is Wilbert, Wilbert Williams."

"Wilbert, you from some parts of Georgia?"

He gave me a strange look and said, "Naw, like I said, I'm a traveling man. Mostly traveled around up north. Been nearly everywhere a man would want to go up there. You name it, mostly been there."

I started to walk up the steps and stopped.

"Where is your family from, Boy?'

He squinted his eyes and said, "Mostly up north, no family down here that I know of. You sho asking me a lot of questions mister. Are you the man I need to be talking to about working here or not?"

I looked over at him and put my hand out.

"Wilbert, my name is BoHenry Johnson." Yea, I'm the man running this place. I don't own it, just running it. Come on inside and get out this hot sun."

I unlocked the door, and Wilbert walked in. He started to look around checking the place out. Wilbert sat on the bar stool and said, "This a nice place you got here mister."

"Thanks, the crowd has really picked up in here, and I guess I could use the extra help."

I turned to Wilbert and said, "You want something to drink boy?"

"Do you have an ice cold beer over there? It's too early and too hot for anything else."

I got the beer and sat it down on the bar. He just stared at it and started rubbing the bottle up and down. He held his head up and said, "So are you gonna give me some work here or not?"

"Have you ever worked in a place like this before?"

"Mister, work is work! As long as you get the job done."

I started smiling and said, "I tell you what, I usually open around six, you come back here around five thirty and I'll show you what needs doing. You let me know if you want to do it, then if you want the job it's yours."

Wilbert jumped up from the bar stool with a big smile on his face and said, "Aight, I'll be back."

He grabbed the beer bottle and drunk the last of it and let out a loud burp and smiled. He headed for the door and then turned around and said, "Thanks for the beer boss man, see ya at five thirty."

"Don't thank me, it's gonna come out your first pay if you take the job. If not, you gonna owe me."

Wilbert started laughing really hard. I could still hear him laughing after he had walked out the door.

I sat at the bar thinking, "Now that's a nice respectful young man there."

Sho nuff at five thirty, Wilbert showed up ready to work. He started telling me how he was gonna prove himself. I showed him the back room with all the supplies and told him, "If there is anything you need, just get it from here."

While Wilbert was looking in the closet, I was thinking I might need to talk to him about the people that comes in and out of here. They got their minds on only one thing. By him being so young I don't want him to mess around and get himself in trouble.

Wilbert started pulling a broom and a mop from the closet and started cleaning around the bar as if he's had been working here for a long time. I watched him for a spell and I was thinking he looked kinda familiar. By him being so young, I've probably been in Topeka longer than that boy been born. He continued working taking the chairs down from the table and wiping them down.

Later that evening, when the crowd started coming in, the women were staring at Wilbert and asking me "Who's that Bo?"

I kept telling them, they are old enough to be this boy's mama. They would all start to laugh.

Later on, Hattie came in and sat at the bar. She looked around and said, "So that's the young man you were tellin me bout, how he workin out?"

I looked over in his direction then back at Hattie and said, "He's keeping the place clean and hasn't complained not once. Now if I can keep these old hens out of his face, he can do more work."

I turned around and looked toward the door and said "Hattie, look who's coming through the door."

Hattie turned on the bar stool to look over towards the door and said, "Lord, I can't believe it. I thought she was dead. I haven't seen her in so long".

I sat on the bar stool watching Alice as she was looking around the room. She looked right over at me and started coming my way. She walked over to me and spun me around on the barstool. I kept my back toward her, ignoring her. She stood right next to me and bumped me in my side and said, "Hey BoHenry, how you been doing?'

"Hey Alice, where you been hiding?"

Alice looked down at me and shouted in my ear, "Well you know I moved out to the country. Had to get away from some people, you know what I mean."

I continued to keep my back toward her when she leaned over on the back of my head and shouted again, "BoHenry how is that mean wife of yours?"

Bo turned and smiled at Alice and said, "Why don't you ask her?"

I looked down at her and said, "Since she's sitting with her back turned and haven't turned around, I assume she don't want to be bothered."

Bo looked over and said, "Now I ain't gonna get in between you two. Y'all better work this out."

Alice tried to get in front of me by spinning me around by my shoulders, but I pushed my feet against the bar and swiveled in the opposite direction.

"Hattie Mae, I ain't got time to be playing with you girl! Now you turn your ass around and look me in the face."

I didn't move, because I thought it was funny.

Bo was watching us and started laughing.

"Y'all girls in here acting like youngum."

I turned around on the bar stool and gave her a surprised look.

"Girl, I didn't know you were in here. How long have you been here?"

Alice put her hands on her hip and said, "I've got better things to do Hattie, than to play with you."

I finally got tired of playing and knew Alice was getting mad. I turned on the stool towards her and acted surprised,

"Alice, who or what has been keeping you locked away!"

"Now listen at you, you can't wait to get in my business."

I fell out laughin.

Alice looked around the room and spotted Wilbert and turned and leaned over the bar and asked, "Bo, what's that new young thang you got over there?"

"Alice, what you talking about?"

Alice pointing over to Wilbert, and said, "Behind the bar Bo."

"Oh, that's Wilbert, he just started working today. Now Alice don't you go nowhere near that boy. He's just a child."

Alice looked over to Bo and gave him a mean look and said; "Now BoHenry don't let me have to come behind that bar."

Hattie looked up and said, "I thought I remember you telling me you got a man. Ain't heard you mention nuthin bout him, not even his name."

Alice put her hands back on her hips and said, "I don't ask you nothing bout you and Bo's business, so stop trying to get into mind. I haven't seen you in months and the first thing you want to ask me about is my man. You ain't even asked me how I am doin."

I turned around on the bar stool and stood up and looked Alice in the face and said, "Girl you're right, you don't know how much I've missed you. I can tell, you have been doing all right cause you lookin better than ever. Come here girl and give ole Hattie Mae a hug."

Alice huggin me real tight said, "Now that's more like it. That was sweet of you. We have so much catching up to do. I really do miss you girl."

I was thinking, it felt good to hug my old friend again.

CHAPTER 30

That evening when I got home from the Juke-Joint, Jt was waiting up for me.

As soon as I walked through the door he asked me, "Alice, how was the crowd at the Joint?"

"I got a chance to see Hattie and Bo. It was really good to see them."

Jt looked at me as if he wanted to say something. He just stared at me and didn't say anything. I started walking towards the bedroom when all of a sudden he yelled, "Well did you invite Hattie and Bo over or what?"

I stood still in the doorway and yelled back, "Yea, you know as nosey as Hattie is, she said she can't wait to meet you! She said they would come over soon, since they got this young boy helping out up there! His name is Wilbert!"

Jt got really quiet and yelled again, "Alice, who is this Wilbert?"

Jt was really getting on my nerves asking me all these questions. It was getting late and all I wanted to do was go to bed. It would have been easier if he had gone out with me.

"Some young man, BoHenry hired to help him out up there. That's all I know about him."

I thought Jt had settled down since he had gotten quiet. I started changing my clothes when all of a sudden Jt hollered back into the bedroom again, "Alice, I'll come to bed later. I just want to sit out here for a minute."

Jt sat down in the chair and closed his eyes thinking about what Alice had said about Bo and Hattie coming over. He laid his head back on the chair thinking about his plan and fell into a deep sleep.

After it had gotten late into the night, I turned over in bed and noticed Jt wasn't there. I got up and went into the kitchen. I spotted a light on outside in the back shed. I started thinking, "Now did Jt leave the light on out there or what? I know I hadn't been out there."

I went into the living room to see if Jt was still sleeping in the chair. I turned the light on and he wasn't there. I looked around and thought maybe he could have been in the bathroom. I looked in there, but he wasn't there either. I looked all over the house, but I couldn't find him anywhere.

I decided to go back into the bedroom and put on an old pair of slippers and my housecoat. I went back into the kitchen and thought about turning on the kitchen light, but decided not to. I went out the kitchen door down the back steps towards the shed. I knew I didn't have any business out there this time of night. Lord, I should mind my own business and go on back to bed.

I kept walking trying to convince myself to go back into the house, but I just kept walking towards the shed. I even started to walk softly so no one would hear me coming. I got to the shed and peeked inside, but by the window being so dirty I could barely see anything. All I could see was a shadow, a shadow that looked exactly like Jt. I stared and noticed that it was Jt.

"Now what in the world is Jt doing out here this time of the night?"

I started to go to the front of the shed door to ask him what he was doing, but just when I got ready to move away from the window, I noticed he was digging or making a hole. This just wasn't making any sense to me. I decided to watch him, trying to understand what he was doing. I felt funny peeking through the window, sneaking and being nosey. I stayed out there till my feet started getting cold. I gave up and decided to make my way on back up to the house.

My mind was so heavy thinking about Jt. I got into bed, knowing I wouldn't be able to sleep. I laid there tossing and turning waiting on him. He stayed out there for what seemed like hours. I thought about getting back up and going out there and asking him, "What in the world are you doing out here this late at night."

I laid there thinking, with all kind of thoughts running through my head.

I finally heard the back door slam, and his footsteps coming towards the bedroom. I didn't know if I should play like I was asleep or not. I was listening for him when I heard him go into the bathroom and the water running. He stayed in there for a good while, and when he came out he went down the hall into the bedroom. I still played like I was asleep when he leaned over and kissed me on the forehead. After he got into bed, he snuggled up under me and I could feel him still breathing hard from digging. As soon as he got comfortable he started snoring. I laid there still awake. My mind was still heavy when I fell into a deep sleep.

The next thing I know, Jt was waking me up telling me he was getting ready to leave for work. I was still half asleep when I said, "Baby, have a nice day and don't work to hard."

He smiled and looked at me really strange and said, "I love you Alice."

I thought that was odd because he has never told me he loved me before leaving for work. I opened my eyes and looked up at him and asked, "Jt, are you all right?"

He smiled and said, "Yea, I'm fine," and walked out the door.

CHAPTER 31

❁

I was glad BoHenry had hired me to help him out at the Juke-Joint. I really enjoyed talking to him. BoHenry liked to talk and I didn't mind listening. He would always tell me about things he had done in his past. I found out he was really an interesting man.

After about three months of working for him, I found out all I needed to know.

One Saturday night after everybody had left the Juke-Joint, Bo and I started cleaning up the place and stacking beers in the coolers. I looked over to him and said, "Bo, I'm surprised after all this time that you haven't figured out who I am."

Bo looked at me with this strange look on his face.

"Wilbert, what you mean figure out who you are?"

I walked over to him so he could get a closer look at me and whispered in his ear.

"Let me let you in on a little secret. I was born on the south side of Chicago, and I'm the youngest of seven. Well it used to be eight, but my sister got killed."

I looked in Bo's face to see if his expression had change, but he just looked at me. I stared at him and said, "Now Bo, does any of that sound familiar to you?"

He put his hand up to his head thinking about what I had just said. A while passed when Bo raised his head.

"Wilbert, I don't know nuthin bout what you talking about, or what you trying to say."

I started getting agitated with Bo, and started pacing back and forth. I looked at him and said, "Now listen you old fool. Didn't you tell me you used to live in Chicago?"

"Yea, I told you that, but watch how you talking to me boy. You better mind your manners!"

I kept looking at Bo and he had this look on his face as if he just couldn't understand what this was about.

"Now listen boy, I don't have all night to try to read your mind. If you got something to say, then say it."

I got up closer to Bo and said, "Well I guess you wouldn't know or figure it out since it's been so long ago. Okay Bo, I am gonna help you out. Let me start at the beginning, I had a sister name Sophie, Sophie Williams. Now Bo, does that name rings a bell to you?"

Bo backed up from me.

Hearing that name made him nervous because he knew one day he would have to face up to his past. He knew Sophie had a lot of brothers and he wouldn't get away with killing her.

I had tears in my eyes when I looked over at Bo because he looked so pitiful.

"Now Bo, do you know who I am? So much time has passed, but it took me this long to find you. I promised my brothers I would find our sister's killer."

Bo just stood there like he couldn't move.

"How could you take my sisters life? She was like our mother. She was all we had and yea you took her away from us. Now I am gonna take your life away from you just like you did hers."

Bo jumped back and started shaking and said, "Boy, you don't have to do this. Don't make the same mistakes I've made! It will be something you have to live with for the rest of your life. You don't know what you doing boy! You are young, and killing is wrong. Don't do this! You don't understand about Sophie and me. I loved Sophie and I don't think I have ever gotten over her. She was the only woman I have ever truly loved. I really loved your sister and wanted to spend my whole life with her."

I looked at Bo with tears running down my face and said, "All I know is you took my sister away from us. You didn't have to kill her, you just didn't! What did she do that was so bad that you had to end her life? She was the only mother we had."

Bo turned and looked out into the bar as if he wished somebody was there. He was looking around for somebody to help him. Bo turned back to talk to me and jumped when he saw I was holding a gun. I was pointing it directly at him. Bo was scared and backed up a couple of steps and was trying to say something. He just busted out crying telling me I don't have to do this. I started thinking about all the time I had spent with Bo. I liked him and knew I couldn't go through with this now.

I started to lay the gun down on the bar when I heard a loud noise. It was so loud it scared me. I jumped, because I didn't realize I had pulled the trigger. I stared at Bo, because I didn't understand what had happened. I watched him fall to the floor. Blood started coming out of his chest. He was panting and looking directly at me. I knelt down beside him and looked him in the face and started yelling.

"Bo, I'm sorry, I didn't mean to do this! It just slipped! I didn't know if I could go through with this after getting to know you."

I just stood there and watched him. It was nothing I could do.

"I guess since it's done, this is for Sophie and she can rest now."

I couldn't take my eyes off Bo. I had never killed anybody before, and never wanted to do it again. He looked really pitiful to me lying there. I started to feel sorry about what I'd done. After getting to know him, I really didn't want to go through with killin him. I noticed tears were starting to run down the side of his face, but it was too late. I stood up and watched Bo lying there on the floor.

Bo started talking about how sorry he was about the things he had done wrong in his life and was asking the Lord to forgive him. He started mumbling something under his breath, I couldn't understand. Then he started another sentence but he didn't finish it. I watched him until he took his last breath. Blood was everywhere. I realized I had started to cry. I didn't know if I had done the right thing or not. I looked around the bar and walked over to the cash register and took everything out of it, even the change. I was thinking about trying to make it look like a robbery, but I didn't want to mess up the place.

I knew Bo kept money in the safe, but I didn't know how to open it. I continued to clean up the place and after everything was done, I turned and looked at Bo on the floor. I knew he was good and dead because he wasn't moving. I turned off the lights and locked the door behind me. I walked down the steps and that was the last time I ever stepped foot in Topeka, Georgia.

CHAPTER 32

I kept gettin up all through the night. I was tossin and turnin and just feelin restless, like sumethin was wrong. I looked around the room to see if Bo had made it home yet, but he hadn't. I thought it was strange for Bo not to be home, since Wilbert had started workin there. Bo always came home early because Wilbert closes the place. I waited up for Bo until I felt sleep comin my way. All through the night I was restless. When I woke up the next time, it was near daylight and Bo still wasn't home.

Since I had been married to Bo he has never stayed out all night. I'm tellin you, sumethin just didn't feel right. My soul was tryin to tell me sumethin. I got up and got dressed. I couldn't lay there any longer when my mind was so heavy. I got up and cooked myself somethin to eat. I knew my Bo would be walkin in the house any minute now, and when he comes in, I'm gonna lay into him sumethin terrible. Got me worryin all about him for nuthin.

Sittin at the kitchen table, I made up my mind, after I finish eatin, I was gonna walk right up to the Juke-Joint to give Bo a piece of my mind. I got myself situated and got out the house. It was barely mornin and the sun was already up. It was so hot. I was walkin and sweatin like a pig goin to the slaughterhouse. I finally made it up to the Juke-Joint, and went right up to the door and turned the knob, but the door was locked. I yelled out for Bo, but he didn't answer. I banged on the door really hard but nobody opened it. I yelled again and thought to myself, "Where in the hell is he?"

I went around to the side of the building and tried to look into the window but the window was too high. I tried to jump up, but this damn weight was just too much to lift off the ground. I kept jumpin up and down as long as I could, then I said, "Good Lord, I got to stop doin this. My heart bout to come right through my chest. Look at me; I can't even catch my breath. I don't think Bo is up here no way."

I just didn't know where he was, and I ain't got no idea where that boyWilbert lived. I went around to the front of the building and just sat down on the steps tryin to figure out what my next move was gonna be.

I was sittin and thinkin, "Suppose if Bo don made it home. I know he's gonna be wonderin where I'm at.

I got up and started home. When I got there, I could tell Bo hadn't been there because everything was still the way I left it. I went into the kitchen and nuthin had been moved. I started sweatin all over again and gettin really nervous, thinkin nuthin but bad thoughts. I knew then sumethin wasn't right. I turned around and walked out the front door down the steps to look for my Bo. I didn't know which direction to go in, so I just started walkin towards Bertha and John Lee's house. When I walked passed their house, I thought I would check and see if JohnLee or Bertha had seen my Bo this mornin. I walked up on the steps and stopped. I couldn't remember what I was comin here for. I didn't have any idea what I was doin. I knocked on the door, but no one came. I knocked harder when Bertha finally opened the door. I just stood there and didn't say a word. Sweat was just pourin off my face, and my heart was beatin like crazy. I felt as if I had been runnin a race.

Bertha looked at me and yelled, "Hattie baby what's wrong!"

I tried to say sumethin, but my mouth wouldn't move. I felt hot all over. All I needed was a little time to sit down, maybe rest for a spell, or just get a cold glass of water.

Bertha looked at me really strange and said in a low voice, "Hattie baby, please tell me what's wrong?"

I looked at Bertha and all of a sudden my knee's got weak. I was tryin to be strong but I couldn't, so I just let it all go. I couldn't hold on no longer. I started goin down to the floor and Bertha was tryin to hold me up. I knew I was too heavy for her. I could hear Bertha screamin my name. The next thing I knew, I was lyin flat on the floor, and could see and hear everything Bertha was sayin, but I just couldn't speak.

JohnLee hearin all this commotion ran into the room, and ask Bertha, "What in the world is goin on? Why is Hattie laid out all on the floor?"

"JohnLee, I think Hattie's don had a stroke, or sumethin. Go bring me a cold rag to put on her face."

I leaned down and put my face close to Hattie's and whispered, "Hattie baby, I can't understand what you sayin, you keep mumblin sumethin about BoHenry's gon. BoHenry gon where baby? Wake up Hattie and tell me what you're tryin to tell me."

Hattie laid out on the floor thinking to herself, she just needed to sleep for a minute, "Yea, that's exactly what I'll do. I'll shut my eyes for a minute and get a little rest and then maybe I can tell Bertha what's goin on."

I stood up and looked around the room. I needed a place to put Hattie. I looked over to JohnLee and said, "JohnLee, we got to get Hattie off this here floor, help me put her on the couch.

JohnLee looked down at Hattie then back up at me and said, "Bertha, don't you hurt yourself pickin Hattie up. Lord knows she's got some weight on her. I don't know if we can move her. You gonna go and mess yourself up tryin to lift Hattie!"

I gave JohnLee a mean look and said, "Now JohnLee you listen, we just can't leave Hattie here on dis floor! Now you gon and get the top and I'll grab her by the legs. I think we can get her up on the couch."

After tryin three times, we finally got Hattie up on the couch. JohnLee was just starin down at her.

"Gon on back into the bedroom and get a blanket to put over her. She ain't well in no shape or form."

JohnLee went back into the bedroom and came out with a blanket and putted it over Hattie.

"Lord, I don't know what's goin on. All I know is she keeps sayin sumethin about BoHenry's gon. You think you ought to go and let Bo know what's goin on over here? If you can't find Bo then gon on down to Pearlie's and let her know."

"Well, let her get some rest now and if she doesn't feel better when she wakes up, I'll go and get Pearlie."

I just stared down at Hattie, because I didn't have any ideal what was goin on. Lord knows, I didn't know what to do.

Hattie laid on the couch all day and didn't wake up once.

I got up early the next mornin to look in on Hattie. I looked down at her and she was still sleepin hard. I started to feel sorry for her, thinkin this woman has really been through some rough times in her life. She looked like she was sleepin as if she wished she wasn't the person whom she had become.

After checkin in on Hattie I went into the kitchen and started to cook breakfast. It didn't take me to long to cook when I started to call for JohnLee to come on and eat. I felt somebody behind me and turned around and Hattie was standin right in the doorway. Hattie looked at me and said, "Bertha, I can't remember much. I don't even know what I'm doin here or how I got over here, but I'm here. How long have I been here?"

I turned around and walked over to Hattie and put the back of my hand on her forehead.

"Baby you sure you feelin better? I don't think you're well just yet. You come on over here and sit down and eat you a little sumethin, then maybe you'll feel better."

I grabbed Hattie by the hand and led her to the table and sat her down. I picked up the plate in front of her and took it over to the stove and came back and sat it down. She looked at it and saw it was some grits, eggs, and salt pork. She looked up to me and said, "Bertha, I don't really feel like eatin just yet, I know you went out of your way, but I just don't feel like eatin."

Hattie kept her head down lookin at the food.

"Bertha I don't know if I don lost my mind or not, but you have to tell me what I'm doin here! Lord knows I can't remember nuthin a t'all!"

I came back over to the table and sat my plate down and started eatin. I looked up at Hattie with a mouth full of food.

"Well you came over here yesterday and knocked on the door. I opened the door and you were standin there with sweat just pourin off ya. You kept standin there mumblin sumethin I couldn't understand. Then the next thing I know, your eyes just rolled back in the back of your head and you passed out in my arms."

Hattie lookin confused, while I just sat there and ate. I looked over to her and asked, "Are you feelin any better this mornin baby?"

Hattie still had her head down and said, "I'm feelin better than I did yesterday I think." Then she looked up and asked, "Did JohnLee let BoHenry know I was over here?"

"I sent him over there yesterday, but BoHenry wasn't at the house."

Hattie started to remember what was going on in her life. She remembered she had not heard from BoHenry and knew within her heart something was wrong and started to cry.

I looked over at Hattie and said, "Hattie baby, what's goin on? "I can't help you if you don't tell me. Maybe you need to lie back down, you'll not that well.

Maybe I should get a doctor to come see bout ya. Maybe I'll send JohnLee for Pearlie. I needs to do sumethin!"

"Now Bertha, I feels just fine. My mind is just too heavy. I got too much on it to carry. My Bo didn't come home to me last night and I've been out lookin for him. Just got tired Bert that's all, Yea, I just got a little tired. Now don't go troublin yourself gettin all worked up over me. I just needs to see my Bo, and to make sure he's all right."

"Well Hattie, I'll have JohnLee to go and look for him so you don't have to go troublin yourself. I told him to go and get Pearlie to come and see bout you if he can't find Bo."

After sittin and eatin, I got up and went to the back door and hollered for JohnLee, "JohnLee! JohnLee, come on in here now!" JohnLee didn't say anything.

I looked back over to Hattie and said; "Now I know that man can hear me callin him.

I called out to him again, JohnLee, I know you hear me!"

JohnLee yelled back, "I hear you Bert, I'm comin. You gots to give me time!"

"Then why don't you answer me like you hear me, you need to act like you got some damn sense."

JohnLee came in through the back door and noticed Hattie standin there behind me and said, "How you feelin this mornin, Hattie? You show gave us a scare yesterday."

Hattie looked away and said, "I'm feelin much better thank you."

JohnLee just stood there. I guess he was waitin for me to tell him what I wanted with him. I turned around and went into the living room. JohnLee followed behind me. When we got out of Hattie's sight, I whispered to him, "Gon on up there to the Juke-Joint and see if you can find Bo. If you can't find him, then gon on down to Pearlie's and tell her to come on up this way to see bout Hattie. Hattie said she hasn't seen or heard from Bo in nearly two days. Now that just ain't like Bo."

JohnLee just stared at me like I was crazy. I just looked right back at him.

"Now Bertha, can all this wait until after I eat my breakfast? Ain't nuthin wrong with Bo, he probably just got tired of Hattie' mess that's all."

I looked JohnLee dead in his eyes and said, "Alright, then come on and eat now fore your food gets cold."

While walkin behind Bertha into the kitchen, I started thinkin bout Bo and all the women that came up to the Juke-Joint. I knew Bo don left Hattie for a young sweet thing. I see how those young girls be lookin and winkin at him.

Hattie turned around and looked at me and said, "Now JohnLee, I know you're gonna look for my Bo. Now if you don't see him up there, make sure you ask around bout him. I know somebody's don seen my Bo. People here too nosey not to have seen him somewhere! Then I guess you should stop by Pearlie's and let her know what's goin on, and where I'm at."

Hattie raised up slowly and looked at me and said, "Now Bertha, I know everything gonna be all right, ain't no need in gettin everybody all worked up over nuthin. I know my Bo is gonna be just fine. I have to put it in the Lord's hand and just keep prayin."

CHAPTER 33

While goin up to the Juke-Joint to look for Bo, I started thinkin about how long Bo and I had been neighbors. Since livin next door, I had never known for Bo to do sumethin like this. Mostly Hattie and Bo just stayed to themselves and minded their own business. They were the strangest people that I knew.

I knew Hattie said she had been up here earlier and didn't see him, but I just wanted to look around and get a really good look for myself, then I'll start lookin somewhere else.

When I got there, I walked up the steps and turned the doorknob, but the door was locked. I pushed against the door and nuthin happened. I pushed harder with my body, and still nuthin happened. I didn't want to break the door so I walked around to the back. It was so much junk on the back porch that I wouldn't even be able to get close to the backdoor. I just stood there lookin at all this junk tryin to figure out what else I could do to get in. I went over to the side window and tried to look in, but the window was too high. I came around and stood on the front porch and started thinkin bout Bo again. I turned around and looked at the door again and said out loud, "Well ain't no way I'm gonna get in there unless I try to break down the front door."

I looked around to see if there was sumethin I could use, but I didn't see anything. I started to run into the door hittin against it with my body. It looked like it wanted to give in a little. I was thinkin, as shabby as this door is it can't keep nuthin out. I kept doin this a couple of times, but nuthin happened. I waited for a minute and then stood back and ran into the door with all my might and the door gave way. I stepped in and looked around and didn't see anybody. I called out for Bo but no one answered. I just stood there lookin. I walked around to the other side of the bar when I saw somebody lyin on the floor. I backed up and looked again. He was lyin on the floor in a pool of blood and I said out loud, "Oh my God! What in the world don happened here!"

I knelt down and touched his neck and tried to wait for his chest to rise, but nuthin happened. I stood up and looked around and didn't see any signs of a fight or anybody else.

Why would somebody do this? Lord, how in the world am I ever gonna tell Hattie this? I just don't think she's strong enough to handle sumethin like this." I needed to get some help.

I got up and went into the back storeroom to see if I could find sumethin to put over him. I couldn't leave him like this. I found an old blanket, and put it over him and just stared at him lyin in all that blood and said again, "Lord, who could have done sumethin like this?"

I started walkin home as fast as I could. When I got to the house, I got up on the porch and tried to listen through the screen door to see if Hattie was still there. I didn't hear anybody talkin, so I walked on in the house. I went to the back of the house into the kitchen and Bert was there makin dinner. She turned around and looked at me and just stood there. She didn't say anything for a long time. I held my head down and said, "I found Bo."

"Well praise God, I know Hattie will be pleased!"

I just stood there not sayin nuthin, not being able to move, because I couldn't tell her what I saw. I stayed there until Bert turned around again and looked me in the face and said, "JohnLee, what's wrong, sumethin not right, is it?"

"I found BoHenry and I don't think he's livin. Bertha, it was so much blood everywhere, ain't no way he could still be livin I tell ya!"

Bertha looked at me strange and said, "Now JohnLee, I ain't heard a word you sayin, I know you can talk louder than that! Tell me what you tryin to say!"

I started talkin louder, "Bert, when I first went up there I couldn't get in. I had to nearly knock the door down. I walked in and called for Bo, but no one answered. I knew sumethin wasn't right. I kept walkin around until I got to the other side of the bar and that's where I found him. Bert I tell you, I don't think he's alive!"

Bertha just busted out cryin then she looked over to me and said "Now JohnLee, Hattie show has been through a lot. I know dis here is gonna send her right over the edge."

Bertha looked up toward the ceilin and spread her arms out wide and said, "Lord have mercy on your child, and help her to be strong. Who could have don sumethin like this?"

She looked over to me. "Lord I just don't know what to do! People are gettin meaner and meaner. People just goin around killin everybody. It's getting mighty bad here, JohnLee. Peoples ain't nice like they used to be!"

I looked over to Bertha and said, "Now Bertha, somebody got to tell Hattie. I think it's only right for you to tell her. It won't look right if I told her, it just won't."

Bertha still cryin, "Well yea, I guess you're right, I don't know if I can be strong for Hattie. I know I couldn't take it if I ever lost you JohnLee. Lord knows I just couldn't take it."

"Now Bertha, you got to get yourself together before you go on over to Hattie's. As soon as she sees you like that, she's gonna know sumethin's wrong."

Bertha looked at me and said, "Well yea, I guess you're right."

She started to wipe the tears from her eyes and said, "All right, just give me a minute."

She went into the livin room and sat down. She sat there shakin her head from side to side tryin to make some sense out of all this. Then all of a sudden she jumped up off the couch and yelled back, "JohnLee, I'm gonna head on over to Hattie's. I know I ain't gon be no mo ready than I am now."

I headed out the door towards Hattie's. While I was walkin I was playin in my mind what I was gon say. I got to the house and walked up the stairs and knocked on the door. No one answered. I waited a minute then knocked again. I heard footsteps comin and knew it was gonna be Hattie. When the door opened it was Pearlie. She just stood there and didn't say anything.

I guess Pearlie had heard bout it through all the talk about Bo bein missin, and came down to see bout Hattie.

Pearlie just stood there lookin at me. She looked me straight in my eyes and didn't even say come in. I guess she figured sumethin was wrong by the look on my face. She turned around and walked back into the livin room and I followed her. She stopped and turned back around and looked at me. I held my head down and asked, "How's Hattie holdin up?"

Pearlie sat down in one of the chairs and said, "Hattie back there in the bedroom lyin down Ms Bert. She hadn't been out of bed all day, and you know that ain't like her. She's not well I tell ya. She just knows sumethin bad has happened to BoHenry."

I sat down in the chair and started tellin Pearlie about how I sent JohnLee to look for Bo, then she cut me off by sayin, "Lord thank you, you tell your husband I thanks him too. Did JohnLee find him?"

I bent my head down and put my hands in my lap and said, "Pearlie, I'm sorry, but I got bad news to give you. "Yeap, JohnLee found Bo up there at the Juke-Joint but sumethin bad had happened. He said he found Bo lyin behind the bar on the floor, and he doesn't know if he's alive or dead. He got a bunch of men goin up there right now so they can make some sense out of all this. I think JohnLee said it looked like he was shot or sumethin."

Pearlie stood up and staggered backward. Tears started to run down her face. She put both hands up to her mouth and started cryin. She was tryin to keep Hattie from hearin her. She ran out the front door and stood on the porch and just let it all out. I went out on the porch after her and held her in my arms while she was cryin until she was strong enough to go back inside. We went back inside and she sat down on the couch and just started cryin again, rockin back and forth.

"Ms. Bert, I've got to be strong for Hattie cause she's not at her best. She's not strong at all."

All of a sudden Hattie came into the livin room and just stood there. She looked over to Pearlie and then she looked at me and said, "Bertha, what you doin here?"

I stood up and didn't say anything. Hattie looked over to Pearlie and asked, "Pearlie baby, what's goin on? Why you sittin here cryin?"

Pearlie just sat there and Hattie continued starin down at her. I looked over at Hattie and noticed a tear had started to fall down her face. She just started cryin slowly. I sat there and notice everything had gotten really quiet.

Hattie looked over to me and I looked away, then she looked over to Pearlie and said; "Now somebody better tell me what's goin on! Did somebody find my Bo?"

I stood up and looked over to Pearlie, then back at Hattie and said, "Pearlie I'm sorry, but I should go. Let you be with your sister, so y'all can talk."

I walked out the door and started down the steps when I heard Pearlie talkin to Hattie. Then all of a sudden, Hattie started screamin, "No Lord, not my BoHenry! Why Lord, why my Bo?"

I turned around to look back up to the house and the next thing I know, Hattie don busted through the screen door and was out on the porch hollering, "Who could have don something like this to my Bo, he don't mess with nobody! He's a good man Lord, why?"

Pearlie was trying to hold on to Hattie and put her back into the house. But Hattie was moving all around the porch. I stood there cryin while watchin all of this. I could still hear Hattie screamin all the way down the street as I was making my way home. "Lord who would do a thing like that to BoHenry?"

CHAPTER 34

As soon as I knew Jt was good and gone to work, I got up and went back down to the shed. I looked at the door and it didn't have the lock on it. I had always been scared to go inside because I knew snakes and things were in there.

I opened the door and peeked inside. It looked really quiet. I opened the door the rest of the way and walked inside. It was kinda dark, so I went back and propped the door opened with a brick so I could have more light. While I was propping the door, I looked around outside and didn't see anybody, then I turned and looked back inside. I could see a whole lot better now. I didn't want anybody to sneak up on me. I started looking around and it wasn't anything in there but some old furniture and stuff we haven't used since Jt and I started living here. I walked over to the area where I saw Jt digging and looked down on the ground. It was a big piece of black plastic covering the floor. A big brick was on each corner. I guessed it was to hold the plastic down. I looked down at the plastic and my heart started racing. I looked back towards the door thinking somebody else might be out here but everything was still and quiet. I was thinking, "Lord, I can't imagine what's under this plastic."

I went to one of the corners and moved the brick off. I tried to move the plastic back slowly but my hands were shaking. I said out loud, "Suppose if it's somebody dead under here. Lord, I won't be no more good!"

I moved the plastic back a little more and all I could see was an empty hole. I bent down and started pulling the plastic all the way back and noticed it was just a big deep hole. I stood up and said, "Thank God, It's nobody under here. I would've just laid down and had a fit."

I put both hands on my hips and just stared at the hole. I was trying to understand why Jt would be digging a hole and what he planned on doing with it?

I looked back toward the door because something just didn't feel right. Suddenly I felt as if I wasn't alone. I turned around and all of a sudden I could see this shadow standing there. I just stood there. I didn't know what to do. I tried to adjust my eyes and I could tell that it was a man.

I yelled out, "Who's there, I can see you so you better say something!"

The shadow came up closer to me and I could see it was Jimmy. I got up on him and said, "Boy, what you doing out here? You scared the living daylights out of me. You almost made me have a heart attack."

Jimmy looked at me with this strange look on his face.

"Ms. Alice, something bad has happened to Uncle Bo! A_nt Hattie is calling for you. She keeps calling your name. You need to come quick!"

I looked down at him and said, "Jimmy how did you get out here?"

He was just sweating all over and said, "I walked, I walked all the way here."

I pushed Jimmy back out of the shed and said, "Now tell me what you trying to say boy."

"Ms. Alice, I said something has happened to Uncle Bo and A_nt Hattie is calling for you! She said she wants you to come right away!"

I was caught off guard and said, "I don't have no car and I show can't walk all the way down to the bottom. What does she want and what's happened to Bo? Lord, I can't do nothing out here. I tell you what, let me go in the house and get dressed, so we can figure out what's going on here."

I looked over to Jimmy and said, "Come on boy, come on in the house."

Jimmy started into the house and stopped short of the door.

"Are you coming in or not?"

He stood there with his head down.

"Ms. Alice, I'll rather stay out here. I'll just sit here on the steps if it's okay with you."

I turned and looked at him and said, "Sit where you want to sit, don't matter to me none."

I started thinking about BoHenry wondering what in the world don happened? What has Bo done got himself into?

I started getting dressed and humming to myself, time passed and I almost forgot Jimmy was outside. I walked out the front door onto the porch and said, "Jimmy, tell me what you said happened to BoHenry?"

"Ms. Alice, I don't know what happened. All I know is, I was told by mama to come down here and get you. I guess A_nt Hattie will tell you everything if we ever get there. She's really upset. Ain't never seen her this upset before."

I looked up across the field and said, "Come on, let's walk up to the store. We should be able to find a ride from there."

We started walking down the street towards the store. Cars were just passing us by.

I looked over to Jimmy and said, "Now I know some of these people knows me. It's too hot to be walking out here."

Jimmy didn't say anything. He just kept walking. As soon as we got to the corner store, I ran in and brought Jimmy a cold soda. I came outside and looked over to him and said, "You know anybody who can give us a ride?"

Jimmy looked up at me and didn't say a word. We both stood outside waiting on the first ride that came along. I started getting tired of standing and looked over to Jimmy and said, "Lord, I sho hope somebody come soon. Lord's know it's too hot to be standing out here."

As soon as I said that a car pulled up. I was staring at the driver because he looked familiar. As soon as he got out the car I started yelling, "Blue, Blue, I thought that was you! Lord, sho glad you showed up. I need a ride down to the Bottom."

Blue looked over to Jimmy and then back at me.

"I was heading down that way, have to run in the store for a minute. Y'all gon and get in the car, I'll be right back. Gon and get out this hot sun."

I opened the car door and pulled the front seat up. Jimmy crawled into the back and I let the seat go hitting Jimmy and knocking him down. He didn't know what to say, he just looked at me. He knew I was upset with him about telling my business.

Finally, Blue came out of the store carrying a brown paper bag. He pulled open the car door and got in and hand a bag to me. I looked down in the bag and said, "I hope you bought one of these beers for me."

He turned and smiled and said, "Now since you need a ride to the Bottom, you're being nice to me. I always see you up there at the Juke-Joint and you barely give me the time of day or say a word to me."

Blue started driving. I was really happy to be getting a ride. I don't think I could have taken too much more of that sun. It was just too hot. Blue looked over at me and smiled so I started to smile.

"Go on you can have a beer."

He leaned toward me and started talking low.

"Tell me Alice, how come I don't see you up at the Juke-Joint like I used too? You got a man that's keeping you in?"

I turned around in the seat and smiled.

"Yea Blue, I got a man, a good man."

He started smiling and leaned back towards the door, and started talking louder.

"I knew something was keeping you in. You know Alice, you a fine sista and when you get tired of him you come and look ole Blue up, aight?"

I started to laugh and said, "All right Blue I hear you talking."

We finally got to the Bottom and Blue turned to me and said, "Where do you want me to drop y'all off?"

I touched Blue on the knee.

"You can drop us off anywhere, we here now."

Blue pulled over and stopped the car. I got out and Blue got out as well and said, "Alice, come over here for a minute and let me holler at ya."

I walked to the other side of the car and Blue whispered in my ear. I laughed and started walking down the road to Hattie's. I wasn't thinking about Jimmy being with me, listening to ole stupid Blue talking trash. I looked back and Jimmy was trying to push the seat up and was reaching for the door handle. He finally got out the car and thanked Blue for the ride. I just kept walking and didn't even look back.

We finally got up to the house. Pearlie opened the door and told me Hattie was in the back bedroom lying down. Pearlie turned around and sat down on the couch and told me to go on back to the bedroom. I thought that was strange for Hattie to be lying down in the middle of the day. I knew something wasn't right. When I got to the bedroom, I stopped at the door and I could see Hattie sitting on the bed crying and rocking back and forth. She had her back turned towards me. I knew something was really wrong because it takes a lot for Hattie to cry. I went into the room, and Hattie turned around and looked at me. She got up and ran over to me and yelled, "Alice, somebody don killed my Bo!"

I couldn't believe what she said. I looked directly at her and yelled, "Hattie, what you saying, tell me what you saying Hattie!"

Tears started to fall down my face. I couldn't believe what she said. She started telling me something about how Bo didn't come home and how she went looking for him. I couldn't understand anything she was saying after hearing her says somebody had killed Bo.

I grabbed Hattie by the arms and led her back to the bed. I sat her down and said, "Hattie, start over and tell me slowly what happened. She started from the beginning and told me everything. I sat there numb. I had all these questions in my head but still I didn't know what to say. We sat on the bed and just started to cry. I held Hattie in my arms until she fell asleep. My heart went out to Hattie. I couldn't understand BoHenry getting killed. Now if it was Hattie that would have been a different story. Pearlie came into the room and sat on the bed. She grabbed Hattie's hand and start patting it. I looked over to Pearlie and said, "Pearlie, if there's anything you need, you send Jimmy for me. Since Hattie's sleeping I'm gonna leave so she can get some rest. I just can't believe this about Bo."

I knew she needed some time to be alone to deal with her loss.

Everybody who came to the Juke-Joint was at the funeral. It was really crowed. Rumors were going around about Wilbert, because he hadn't been seen or heard from since the day Bo was killed. Nobody knew anything about him, if he was dead or alive, or if he had done it or not. He didn't even show up for the funeral, and everybody thought that was strange.

It had been about a month since BoHenry's death. Hattie still hadn't gotten any better. The law came out to investigate it but as long as it's another black killing another black, they said they couldn't find a crime in that. Hattie wasn't the same after Bo's death. She spent a lot of time to herself. She said, she would find out who killed her Bo or die trying. She became meaner and meaner, and started to hate everybody. Nobody could say anything to her but Pearlie. Even me and Jimmy kept our distant.

After about three month of Bo's death everything had calm down a bit. I decided to go and check on Hattie. I got to the house and Hattie opened the door. I didn't say anything, I just stared at her to see if she looked the same or what. She looked at me and said, "Alice, it's really good to see ya. Come on and let's go back to the bedroom so we can talk. We sat down in the bedroom and I looked over to Hattie and said, "Hattie you looking really good. How you been doing?"

She held her head down and said, "Alice, I'm tryin to make it day by day. I don't know why the good Lord took my Bo. He didn't deserve this. Ain't been able to get a good night rest since this all happened. Sometimes I think I'm bout to lose my mind, tryin to figure this one out."

I didn't know what to say. I held my head down for a minute then I looked back up to Hattie. She was just staring at me like I was crazy and didn't say anything. I tried to stare back at her, but I kept turning my head away. For some reason I felt funny being here. She didn't act the same. I didn't know what to think of this. The room got really quiet, so I started talking about Jt. Hattie seemed like she was really interested in the conversation, so I kept on talking. I started making a little of it up as I went along to make it more interesting. Hattie kept staring at me. I noticed that every time I would talk to her about Jt she would pep up. Hattie looked over to me and said, "Girl, I'm tired of you talking about this man. When am I gonna meet this new man of yours, huh?"

I looked at Hattie and said, "You'll meet him in due time. It'll be soon."

Hattie needed something to take her mind off BoHenry. She didn't talk about missing Bo too much, but I knew she did. She wasn't one to show any weakness.

One day while I was visiting Hattie, we were sitting and talking about my relationship.

"Alice, what's the name of your make believe man?"

I looked at her and said, "What do you mean make believe? I got a real man Hattie."

That got me so mad I just blurted out!

"For your information, his name is Jt, Jt Hattie! Now are you satisfied?"

Hattie smiled knowing she had gotten the best of me, and said, "Jt? What kind of name is that for a man? He must be a child."

I got really pissed off and said, "He's a long way from being a child, this is a good man, and yes Hattie, he's my man, yes my man! Now what you got to say about that!"

Hattie started laughing, but I didn't see anything funny. After I knew Hattie had gotten the best of me, I felt bad for telling her Jt's name.

She started mocking me saying "Jt, Jt." She had this strange look on her face and she seemed disturbed. Then all of a sudden she told me that I had to leave because she had something to do and was forcing me out the front door. I thought it was strange. I thought I had said something to upset her, but all I said was, my man's name was Jt.

When I got home that evening, Jt asked me about Hattie, about how she was doing since losing BoHenry. I told him Hattie was doing fine and we talked a lot about him every time I went there.

"Have Hattie ever asked you my name?"

"Yea, she asked me today, and I told her."

Jt sat up from the chair. I knew he was gonna be mad.

He just stared at me but he didn't get upset.

"Why would you do something like that Alice? I told you I didn't want people knowing my business. I did tell you that, right?"

I held my head down and said, "Jt, she got me so mad I just told her."

He turned around with his back toward me. He looked like he was thinking about something. He turned back around to me and said, "Well what did she say after you told her my name?"

All these questions started getting the best of me so I said, "Jt, is there something you need to tell me about Hattie? She seems to want to know everything about you and all you want to do is know everything about her. What's going on here?"

He smiled and said, "Trust me Alice, I will tell you all you need to know soon enough."

I turned and walked into the kitchen, and Jt went back into the living room and sat in his chair. After about ten minutes he walked back into the kitchen and stood behind me and put his arms around me and said, "Alice, I tell you what. Why don't you invite Hattie over? I think it's time you start introducing your man to your best friend. What do you think about that? You don let the cat out the bag, so you might as well have her on over here."

I turned around in Jt's arms facing him.

"Do you mean we can start going out, going up to the Juke-Joint, or anywhere we want together?"

I looked Jt in the eyes and said, "I really do love you. I love you so much Jt. I have been waiting for this day to come for so long."

I started thinking about Hattie coming over and finally meeting her face to face. I didn't know if I had changed a lot, or if Hattie would recognize me. How could she not recognize me with this patch over my eye? It would all come back to her.

I knew it was time to put my plans to work. I didn't care about her being in pain from losing BoHenry. She left me for dead, and I've been thinking about it every day since I've set foot here in Topeka. I can't wait to put all this into motion.

CHAPTER 35

I started makin changes in the house. I didn't like the things that I used to like since BoHenry was gon. I wanted to move away, but I knew I had gotten to old to be tryin to make changes to a new city. I was gonna have to make due right here in Topeka. I just can't keep runnin from life. I've gotten too old.

I knew things were different now. People started treatin me differently. They act like they didn't want to be bothered with ole Hattie Mae anymore. Some would even try to disrespect me but I wasn't gonna settle for that. I hated to go back to my old ways. I've been doin good turnin over my soul and all I want, is to be left alone. Have some peace and quiet in my life, but I don't think they gon let me. Wherever I go, trouble just ain't far behind me.

Since Bo was gone there was no money comin in. I ain't worked in so long. Can't remember the last time I've worked. I've gotten too old and too settled in my way to be tryin to be dealin with them anyway.

After thinkin about ways to get some money, I decided to ask the owner of the Juke-Joint if I could take over Bo's old job. The Juke-Joint had been shut down for a while and it wasn't doin nuthin no way. I knew I could make some good money and pay some of these bills that was addin up.

After thinkin bout it for a couple of weeks, I decided to walk on up there to see what type of shape the place was in. I walked all the way up there in the hot sun and got up the first two steps and my feet just stopped. I tried with all my might, but I just couldn't move. "Lord' what don happened to me?"

Ain't been up here or passed by here since my Bo was killed. The first thing that came to mind is, I was havin another stroke. I just stood there and waited a second before I tried to move again. I made it up on the porch and reached for the doorknob and turned it, but the door was locked.

I decided to walk on over to the owner house to speak to him bout tryin to run the place. The owner was an old white man who lived with his wife in a big ole house not to far down the road from the juke-joint. I finally made it up to his house and knocked on the door. He looked out and told me to go round to the back. He came around to the backdoor and looked me up and down and said, "What do you want, girl?"

I told him I was BoHenry Johnson's wife. He looked at me with a frown on his face and said, "Who in the hell is that?"

I told him that he was the one who was runnin the Juke-Joint and got killed up there. I knew he had heard about it.

He looked up at me and said, "Oh, well what do you want, I ain't got no money?"

I started tellin him what I was doin there and what my plan was. After we talked about it, we both agreed we could use the money. He gave me the key and made sure I knew, I was gonna have to be responsible for whatever happened there. He started to walked into the house and turned around and asked, "How you feel bout the place since your husband was killed there?"

I looked at him and said, "Well he's dead now and workin up there ain't gonna make him any deader."

I thanked him again, and went on home. I didn't feel like walkin back over to the Juke-Joint. It was just too hot. I felt I had done enough for one day.

When I finally got home, there was a man standin on my front porch. I knew it was a bill collector, so I went around to the back of the house and came in through the woods. I got inside the house and I could still see the man sittin on my porch. "Lord, I ain't got no money just yet, what am I gonna tell this man?" I went to the front door and opened it. The man turned around, and asked, "Are you Hattie Johnson?"

I held my head down so he couldn't see my eyes, cause I know I was bout to tell a lie. I thought about it and decided not to, so I just said, "Yea."

He looked me up and down and said, "How you doing? I'm BoHenry Johnson's brother, my name is Staley."

I started to smile and said, "Lord Staley, what you doin down here in these parts of the woods?"

"I'm sorry to be sitting on your front porch, but I didn't know where else to go since I just got into town this morning. I asked around bout you to find out where you live. I hope you don't mind me sitting out here?"

I was still surprise, and asked, "Have you been sittin out here all day?"

Staley smiled and said, "Yes ma'am, I guess I have."

I looked back into the house and said, "Well come on in here so I can get you some cold water."

He walked in and looked around. I sat down on the chair and told him to sit down. We just stared at each other.

"Well Hattie, I know you're wondering why I'm here."

I was starin at him while he was talkin.

"I got wind of my brother's death and I'm sorry I didn't make it to the funeral. I got down here as fast as I could. I came down to get the rest of his belongings and to see what it is I could do to make you feel more comfortable."

I just sat there lookin, and listenin. He was lookin at my expression and knew I had no ideal what he was tryin to say.

"Hattie, I have been tryin to get out of Chicago for a long time and I guess it took my brother's death to get me moving. Didn't know if I wanted to come to the south or not, but here I am."

I really didn't know what this man was talkin about so I just came out and asked, "Well how long you plannin on stayin here? BoHenry didn't have much belongin, and I don't know nuthin bout his insurance."

"Hattie, I didn't come down here to try to start no trouble with you. I don't care about no insurance or anything. I was looking around when I came in on the bus and thought that this would make a good little place for me to make a new start. The air is nice here and I ain't got to hear all that city noise. It's much nicer down here in the south; plus I need a break from Chicago."

"Well Staley, where you gonna stay?"

He looked around the room then back at me.

"Well I ain't thought much about that."

I was still confused.

"Well Staley, I don't know you from a man in the moon. I know you say you're BoHenry's brother. I've heard him talk about you and all, but I've never met any of ya. I don't know if I can have a strange man stayin in my house by me livin here alone and all.

Staley smiled again and said, "I was looking around town, and thought I could find me a little place to lay my head for awhile, then when and if you feel comfortable with me, then maybe you'll have a little room I could rent from you. I know you could use some extra money, now that Bo's gone. I know you're lonely and thought that maybe you could use a little company. I'm a really good handy man and if it's anything needs fixin, then maybe I could do it for you."

I just sat there listening and staring. I had no ideal who this man was or what he was trying to say. I sat there thinking, "Lord, what's gonna happen next?"

CHAPTER 36

I was still keeping my eyes and ears open when it came to Hattie. I knew BoHenry's brother was stayin at Hattie's house, but I had no ideal who he was and really didn't care. I started to watch her closer because I knew time was running out and I was ready to put my plan into action.

When I got off work, I would swing down to the Bottom to see if I could run into Hattie. I was always hoping and waiting for something to happen, but nothing ever did.

Sometimes I would catch her going in and out of her place and I would just sit there and watch her for hours at a time. I knew it would only be a matter of time before we came face to face. It was hard for me to keep it a secret that I was here. I just wanted to walk up to her and let her know I had found her.

Every time I went into the Bottom, I prayed that Hattie would look my way and recognizes me, but she never did. I even tried to let her see me watching her, but she paid no attention to me. She just went on about what she was doing. I had hatred in my heart for Hattie. I've never understood how she could say she loved me and then try to kill me at the same time, then she just leave me for dead.

It's been a lot of years since that happened. I know I should let it go, but Hattie broke my heart. When you break a man's heart, it's a terrible thing. I don't think you can move forward till you settle the score. Ain't never loved like I love Hattie. Hattie was my first love and I picked her over my family. Now I don't have either. All this was going through my head while I was sitting out here watching her.

CHAPTER 37

I finally opened the Juke-Joint back up and the people started comin in. I knew they would come because they didn't have any other place to go to get drunk. At first it wasn't as crowded as it used to be, but I enjoyed workin there anyway. It just reminded me a lot of Bo. Some of the customer would say to me, "Hattie, you don't mind workin here after what happened to your husband?"

I would mostly just smile and say, "I'm alright."

I started to work the Juke-Joint all by myself, but when the crowd got bigger I knew I was gonna need me some help. I was too old to be tryin to do all this by myself, but Lord knows I needed the money. Being here all times of the night, I knew I would need me some protection too, plus they were startin to get rowdy. On some nights they would get out of control, and I was havin a hard time breakin them up. I needed a man in here with me. Some people thought I had lost my nerves. They thought I had gotten a little soft, since I had lost my Bo but they had another thing comin.

One night, while I was workin that man every body calls, "Never Tremble" got really drunk. I tried to put him out the bar by pullin on his shirt. I didn't want to embarrass him, so I did it kind of nicely. Do you know, he looked me right in my eyes and drew his hand back and slapped me in the face with all his might, right in front of everybody?

He started yellin, "Get your goddamn hands offa me. You don't know me like that heffa! I'll kill you if you ever touch me again!"

He was just causin a big scene. Everybody in the bar got quiet and backed up. They were waitin to see if ole Hattie don lost her nerves. I calmly let go of his shirt and reached in my bra and pulled out old faithful so fast, Never Tremble didn't even see it comin. He didn't even know I had a knife up to his throat till I put pressure on it. I wanted to let him know I wasn't playin with him. He felt that blade and realized I didn't mind takin his life away.

He started to laugh real loud and said, "Ole Hattie, you still got it. I didn't see you pulled that knife on me. Don't cut me, I'll leave."

I pulled him closer to my face and said, "Never Tremble, if you ever disrespect me again in your life, I'll cut you so short, you'll have to be buried in a baby's casket. That's your final and only warnin. Now make sure you heard me and heard me good, all right?"

He pushed back from me and said, "I hear you Hattie."

He went on out the bar, stumblin down the steps. I went outside on the porch to see where he went. He was headed on down the road towards his house.

He looked back and saw me on the porch and shouted back, "Ole Hattie, one day you ain't gonna be so lucky, somebody gonna get your black ass. Your luck is gonna run out. You're gettin old Hattie."

He turned back around and started walkin, disappearin into the darkness.

Shortly after that incident, I knew I needed some real protection. I got myself a gun. I was thinkin that I needed me a nice pistol that fits really good in my hand, so my aim won't be off. Somethin I can handle easily.

I knew times were gettin bad, so when I walked from the Juke-Joint, I would carry my gun outside my bra. I kept it right in my hand, because it made me fell a whole lot safer.

I remember back in the days when I was a lot younger, about twenty years ago. I would have gon out shootin for no reason at all and trust me, I know I would have hit sumethin. I was meaner than a rattlin snake back then, and some of that meanness is still in me if you bring it out. Lord knows I'm tryin to turn over my soul.

CHAPTER 38

❀

Hattie and I started getting to know each other a little better. I was learning my way around Topeka, Ga. The more I got to know the place, the more I liked it. Whenever she would need some work done around the house she would call on me and I would do it. I could tell Hattie enjoyed having me around, because she would always say, "Staley, you sho do mine me a lot of my Bo. Lord, I sho miss him so much."

One day Hattie asked me, "Staley, how much money you payin over at that boarding house. I know you payin good money."

"Now Hattie, why you need to know that?"

She looked over to me and smile and said, "Well, I could sho use some of that money."

Hattie eyes lit up while she was talking.

"Now you could rent out that ole bedroom in the back if you like. Now if you do, then you gonna have to mind your manners in my house. I ain't never had another man to live with me, 'cept my husbands. That bedroom ain't big, but you ain't gonna be doing little of nuthin in there anyway."

I moved into Hattie's house the following week. I would have move in sooner but I was already paid up for the week at the boarding house. I started going out looking for work every morning. I would get little odd and end jobs and always paid Hattie her rent on time. The rent wasn't as much as I was payin at the boarding house, so I didn't think she was trying to take advantage of me.

One day I came home all happy, telling Hattie I finally got a job working at the tire factory. She was really happy for me and said, "The only way to make a man feel like a man is for em to have they own money. Staley, I'm glad you got a job."

One afternoon Pearlie came by the house to check on Hattie. I just happened to be off work. I heard somebody knocking so I opened the door. Pearlie looked surprised because she didn't have any ideal who was opening her sister's door. She just stood there and didn't say anything, so I asked her, "Ma'am, how may I help you?"

She smiled and said, "Well this is my sister's house and I just came by to see how she'd doing."

"Come on in, my name is Staley, I'm BoHenry Johnson's brother."

Pearlie looked me up and down.

"I'm sorry to hear bout your brother. Are you from Chicago as well?"

I looked at her and noticed she didn't looked nuthin like Hattie. Pearlie was really a beautiful woman with a soft voice and a beautiful body. I couldn't help but stare her up and down. I smiled and said, "Yes ma'am, I'm from Chicago, too. Would you like to come in and sit down?"

Pearlie sat down on the sofa and stared at me. I couldn't believe how beautiful she was. I tried to start up a conversation with her to see if she was seeing anybody, but the conversation wouldn't go that way. Every time I started that way, she would start asking questions about me.

I looked at her and said, "I've always wanted to move down south. I like it down here because people are much friendlier and the crime ain't so bad. So now I'm here, I feel I should at least try to get comfortable and make it my home."

Pearlie started smiling and got up from the chair and said, "It was really nice meeting and talking to you, but I have to go. When Hattie gets home, please tell her I came by. Once again, I'm sorry to hear about your brother."

I got up from the chair and walked Pearlie to the door.

"Ms. Pearlie, it was my pleasure to meet you as well. I'll tell Hattie you came by."

I watched her walk down the street until I couldn't see her anymore. I started thinking about Pearlie as soon as she got out of my sight. Thinking about how nice it would be to spend some quality time with her. I just couldn't believe the difference between her and Hattie. She was really a beautiful woman and I can't wait for Hattie to get home so I can find out as much about her as I can.

After falling asleep on the couch, I heard the screen door slam and woke up. I looked up and it was Hattie. I couldn't help but notice how tired she looked. She looked as if she really had a rough day. I didn't know if it would be a good time to start asking her questions so I just told her, "Your sister Pearlie came by."

When I said that she looked really surprised. She stopped and turned around and said, "Well, did you tell her who you were and what you were doin here?"

I started to smile and said, "Yea, I told her I was BoHenry's brother. She's really a nice looking lady."

Hattie started to walk away when I said, "Hattie, are ya'll really sisters? I mean do ya'll have the same mama and daddy?"

Hattie looked surprise and said, "What you mean askin me sumethin like that. Yea, that's my sister! Why, what you tryin to say?"

I couldn't help but laugh and said, "Well Hattie, how can I get to know your sister a little better? Does she have a man in her life or not?"

Hattie started smiling, so I said, "I want you to tell me all about her. What she likes and don't like. I think I could be really good for her."

Hattie looked as if she was thinking about what I said, then looked back at me.

"Well, I don't know, Pearlie's been without a man for too long. I don't know if you would fit into her plans.

"I'm a good man, a hard worker and I don't think I look that bad either. I think I'm a good catch too. Don't you think so Hattie?"

Hattie started smiling, and said, "Well, you'll have to try to get to know Pearlie on your own, she's a strange one. I don't know if she will let you get close to her. Why don't you just stop by her house and see what fixin up you can do round her place. Ain't no man been there for a long time, so I know she'll like that, also she might welcome your company."

I started thinking about what Hattie said.

"Yea, that's exactly what I'll do."

Hattie started walking down the hall towards her bedroom smiling. Then she said out loud, "God had a funny way of changin people's life."

The next day, as soon as I got off work, the first thing I did was go over to Pearlie's. I was really nervous going up the steps to her house. I got to the door and knocked hard. At first I thought no one was home, because I didn't hear anybody. I waited a little longer when a young boy opened the door. I looked down at him and said, "Hi, how you doing? Is Pearlie home?"

The young man looked up and just stared at me.

"Nope, my mama ain't home yet."

I felt kinda bad walking all this way in this hot sun and she wasn't home. Then in a way I was kinda glad because I didn't know how she would feel about me just up and coming to her house.

"Well do you know who I am?"

Jimmy looked at me and didn't say anything.

"No, I don't think we've met."

I started to turn around and leave, but then I stopped.

"Well I'll be back, so you don't have to tell your mama I came by."

The young man looked surprise and said, "Well who are you?"

"I guess it would help if I told you my name. I'm BoHenry's brother, my name is Staley."

Jimmy opened the door some more and stuck his head out.

"Well my name is Jimmy, and I'll tell my mama you came by."

I watched Staley as he walked up the road until I couldn't see him anymore. I couldn't wait to tell my mom that Uncle Bo's brother came by.

CHAPTER 39

Everybody in town was talking about BoHenry's brother. Alice had gotten wind of it and was wondering what he was doing in town.

She came over to the house and said, "Hattie, I want you to introduce me to BoHenry's brother. I hope he ain't here to start no trouble."

I looked at her and said, "You've been tellin me all this time bout you got a man. Now what happened to him? If he's such a good man then why you need to meet Staley, and no he ain't here to start no trouble Alice, he's a nice man?"

Alice looked over at me and said, "Hattie, the reason I want to meet him is none of your business. Just do what I asked you to do."

I knew in the back of my mind I wasn't ever gonna introduce Staley to Alice. He don't need a woman like Alice.

One day I was thinkin bout Alice and tryin my best to remember the name of the man she said she was stayin with. I couldn't remember that name to save my life. As a matter of fact I hadn't seen Alice since she came over here askin about Staley. I guess she figure I wasn't gonna introduce them, so she had no reason to come back. I wish I could run into her so I can ask her. I knew once the Juke-Joint opened, I would see her there.

I had to get up to the Juke-Joint so I could get it ready to open. It was some things that needed fixin. I ask Staley if he could help me fix up the place a bit. Fix it up so people would come in and have a good time and not worry about somebody fallin thru the floor, or havin rain come in on their heads. I told Staley, when things started pickin up, he could come and work behind the bar with me if he wanted too. It would look good to have a man up in there.

Once people found out the Juke-Joint had reopened they started comin in slowly. I guessed they wanted to see what changes was made and to see if it was safe to come in. Everybody was really scared after BoHenry's death. I was still no closer to findin out who killed him. Wilbert had disappeared like a ghost. When they walked in and saw me runnin it, some of them would just stare at me, or they would say, "Hattie, have you finally lost your mind? Lord, I can't believe you up here after what happened."

I would just look at em and smile. I knew what I was doin. They say the Lord don't put no mo on you than what you can bare.

One Saturday night, the Juke-Joint was packed. I was feelin good bout all the money I had taken in. I didn't know how to use the money safe, so when I walked home in the dark, I had my money in one hand with my pistol in the other. I felt people knew me in these parts and knew better to try to jump me or take my money. I always teased people about how I would shoot first and ask questions later if sumethin ever happened on that dark road.

I had stayed a little bit later than I used to. There wasn't anybody around to walk me home so I started walkin by myself. I always walked fast down that dirt road that lead from the Juke-Joint, because there were no lights on it at all. It was so dark; you couldn't even see your hands in front of your face. Anytime I am out there walkin, I'm always listenin for anything cause like I said, "I'm gonna shoot first and ask questions later."

I was takin it easy like, cause I had a rough night. Sometimes that Juke-Joint just wears me out. I was walkin down the road and heard a strange noise in front of me. I slowed my steps because sometimes a dog or sumethin be walkin on the road. I eased forward and could tell sumethin or somebody was out here. I stopped and listened to see if I could hear anything. I heard it move again. I looked all around me and all I could see was darkness. I was walkin slowly cause I just didn't want to be standin here with sumethin that I didn't know what it was. The closer I got, it looked like I could see sumethin or somebody. I couldn't make heads or tails what it was or who it was, but yea it was sumethin. I squinted my eyes so I could see but I still couldn't tell what or who it was. I yelled out, "Now I know somebody is out here! This is ole Hattie and I don't play out here on this road. It's too dark so you better say sumethin and let me know who you is! I got my stuff with me and I ain't afraid to use it!"

I waited for somebody to say sumethin, but nobody said a word. Then all of a sudden, I heard sumethin move to the side of the road. I could see a shadow, and I could tell it was a person. I still couldn't make heads or tails if it was a man or woman.

I started getting kinda nervous and said again real loud, "Now somebody better tell me who you is, or it's gonna be a lot of trouble out here on this road tonight. Now this is ole Hattie and you know I don't play! I already got my stuff out with my finger on the trigger."

I moved up closer to get a better look or just to try to walk around whatever the hell it was. When I got closer, sumethin hit me right in the face, knockin me backward. I didn't even see it comin. My pistol went one way and my moneybag went the other. All I saw was lights and stars and fell backward to the ground. I started crawlin around tryin to find my gun and my money but I couldn't tell what from what, because I couldn't see nuthin. Then all of a sudden, I felt somethin come across my back knockin me back to the ground. I tried to reach my hands out feelin for my pistol, but all I kept gettin was a handful of dirt and rocks. I started yellin, because the pain was killin me!

"Now stop it, it's me, Hattie! Now you know I don't play! When I get up from here, I'm gonna start shootin till I get tired. I'm gonna kill sumethin tonight."

The board came down across my back again, nearly knockin me out. I tried to get up, but I was hurtin somethin terrible. I manage to get up on one knee, but the board came across my back again and knocked me back to the ground. I couldn't move after that. I just laid flat on that road. Whoever it was, didn't say a word, they just continued to beat me till they got tired and knew, or thought I was dead. I couldn't do nuthin but lay there. I was hurtin and could tell I was bleedin all over the place. I could feel my clothes all wet. I knew it was either sweat or blood. I felt all my feelins leavin me. I knew this person was tryin to kill me so I yelled out, "Lord, please help me!" I tried to look up again to see if I could see who this was, but it was just too dark. All I could tell is that it was a man.

I just laid there not moving when somebody bent down over me and said, "It took me all this time to get to you Hattie, but I finally got your big, black ass! You left me for dead, and that's the same way I am gonna leave you out here on this road. I should just beat you some mo till I know you're dead! Shit, I was hopin you would see me face to face, but here in the dark will do just fine. You don't know who I am do you Hattie? You can't tell my voice? I'm your husband, it's me Josiah, remember me? The one you left for dead after hittin me with that skillet knockin my brains out. I tell you if it wasn't for Roscoe savin my life, no tellin where I might be. It took all I had to get to you Hattie, but I got you now. I've been livin right here in Topeka for a long time now, just waitin on you. Now I am doin exactly what I came here to do, to kill your fat ass."

I knew I was hearin things. It must be my conscious gettin the best of me. I knew the pain was too much and I just couldn't be hearin this right. There was no way Josiah could be in Topeka. How would he even know to come here? He's supposed to be dead. That's been so many years ago. Why was his voice inside my head?

That man started kickin me in the side, and I could feel the pain all the way up to my head. He just continued to beat me with that board and kickin me anywhere he saw fit. All I could do was lay there, cause I didn't have the strength to do nuthin else. I just closed my eyes right there on the side of the road, layin there bleedin to death. I could hear him shoutin sumethin about Alice tellin me he was here. Sumethin about me bein too stupid to put two and two together. All I remember is, I was gettin sleepy and the pain didn't hurt so much. Yea, all I needed was some sleep and some rest and that's exactly what I'm gonna do. I closed my eyes and fell into a deep sleep.

CHAPTER 40

The next day I got up, I noticed Hattie wasn't in the house. That was kinda strange, because since I had been stayin here she had never stayed away from home all night. I didn't know what to think of this. I walked around the house thinking that maybe she came home late and had gotten up really early for some reason to handle some business. I had come to find out Hattie was a strange one. I looked all around for her but she was nowhere to be found. I didn't know what was going on, but I knew I didn't have time to be foolin with her today. I had one thing on my mind and it was gettin to know Pearlie. This was my one-day off and I wanted to spend the whole day with Pearlie. I told Pearlie yesterday I was comin over the first thing in the mornin to start seein what workins she needed doing on that house of hers.

I got dress and started walking toward Pearlie's. I really wanted to impress her and knew if I did a good job fixin on her house that she might take a liking to me.

I started thinking about Hattie again and thought that maybe before I started down to Pearlie, maybe I should go up to the Juke-Joint just to make sure everything was all right. Find out why she didn't make it home last night?

It was really early and no one was out yet. The sun hadn't come up mad this morning and I was hoping to get working before it got too hot. Lord knows it gets hot in Georgia during the summer. I hadn't got too used to this Georgia heat just yet.

I was walkin up the dirt road towards the Juke Joint, and came across sumethin lying on the side of the road. I couldn't really tell who or what it was until I got up close on it. It looked like a person. Whoever it was, they were lying in the bushes all covered with weeds. It looks like they have gotten too drunk to make it home last night.

I walked up closer and looked down. It was so much blood everywhere and knew this person couldn't possibly be alive. I didn't want to get too close, but after looking closer it started to look more and more like Hattie. I started pulling the weeds off of her and I couldn't believe what somebody had done. I looked around and said out loud, "Lord, please don't let this woman be dead! How can somebody do this to her!" Somebody had really messed Hattie up good. How am I ever gonna tell Pearlie about this?

I knew I needed to go and get help, but I didn't know where to go. I didn't want to leave her lying here like this. I wanted to move the body out of the bushes, but I knew I couldn't move her by myself. I looked up and down the road and didn't see a soul. I just stood there and waited.

CHAPTER 41

After Jt got home that evening, I noticed he was really nervous about something. He had changed from his work clothes and was really jumpy. Something just didn't seem right about him. He started rambling about leaving Topeka. He turned and looked at me and said, "Alice if I ask you to move to another town with me, would you? Would you want to leave Topeka?"

I looked up at Jt and asked, "What is this all about? You come in here jumpy, moving back and forth and talking about moving away, now what is this all about?"

Jt just stared at me like I was crazy, so I just blurted out, "I don't know if I feel like moving to another city, we have never talked about it before."

Jt sat down in a chair and put his head down like he was in deep thought. Then he got up and started walkin back and forth, and not saying anything. I just stood there looking at him until I just couldn't take it anymore. I looked at him acting all crazy and said, "Jt, what in the world is wrong? You need to start talking right now!"

Jt stopped dead in his tracks and turned with his back to me and said, "Alice, I think you need to sit down so we can talk for a minute."

I went over to the couch and sat down and Jt started back pacing.

"Alice, I know you think I'm a private person, but I have my reasons for being that way. It's a lot you don't know about me."

He came over to where I was and grabbed me by the hand and led me into the kitchen. I thought this was really strange. We were already sitting in the living room, and now he moves me to the kitchen. He sat down at the table and looked me straight in the eyes and said, "Alice, I know you're not gonna believe this, but I used to be married to Hattie!"

I started laughing because out of all the things he could say, he came up with this. I knew he wasn't telling the truth.

"Now Jt stop playing, if you are gonna be serious, then you need to be serious. I thought you wanted to tell me something."

He grabbed me by the face and turned my head towards him and said, "Alice, I'm telling you the truth, I used to be married to Hattie!"

I looked deep in his eyes and could tell he was serious. I just stared at him and said, "Jt, I can't believe it. How is that possible? What type of damn games are you playing with me? I have been in your life all this time, and now you're telling me you used to be married to Hattie?"

Jt put his hands on my shoulder, but I knocked them off. I looked at him like I wanted to kill him. If I could kill this man and get away with it, I would have done it right then and there.

"Don't try to act like this is a game Jt cause it's not. You better start telling me what you are doing and why you are here. I still can't believe this. You used to be married to Hattie? Okay, why are you telling me this now? Wait a minute! How could you be married to her and she was married to BoHenry?"

Jt got up from the table and turned toward me and said, "Let me start from the beginning. I met Hattie a long time ago, down in Baton Rouge, Louisiana. Oh, that Hattie was something else. She could make a grown man wear a winter coat in ninety-degree weather. I lost my mind over Hattie, couldn't get enough of her."

I was looking at Jt as if he was talking about somebody else.

"Are we talking bout the same Hattie?"

I knew Hattie could never hold a candle to me, but I had never heard a man speak of Hattie in that way. I knew Hattie could keep a man, but I didn't know what Hattie had that I didn't have more of. I just stood there listening to Jt.

He continued talking, "I was young when I met Hattie. We were both in love. One day I just turned around and asked Hattie to marry me and for a time I was really happy. My family tried to talk me out of it, but I had to have her. I don't know what it was about her. Maybe she had roots on me or something, I don't know. We had a lot of good times and not too many bad times, but I guessed I started treating her really bad. She just got tired and tried to kill me. As a matter of fact, she thought she had killed me and left me for dead. If it wasn't for a good friend of mine who found me lying half dead on the floor, I wouldn't be here to tell you this story.

He stood up and turned with his back toward me and continued talking, "I stayed in the hospital for a long time wondering why Hattie never came to see bout me. I never knew she thought she had actually killed me. She just packed up and moved away with me lying on the floor bleeding half to death. I didn't know she could be so hateful and mean. When I got better and out of the hospital, I swore I would find Hattie if it killed me and do the same thing to her."

I stood up and stepped back from Jt listening to his every word. All I heard was something about a lot of killing. I couldn't believe what he was saying, but it started making sense to me now. I started thinking about all the times Jt and I have been together. He always avoided Hattie and BoHenry. He didn't want people to be around us and we never went out together in public. Even when we went to make groceries he wouldn't even go inside the store, he would just tell me what he wanted and I would buy it. No one ever saw us together.

I sat back down, and then I stood up with my hands on my hips and said, "Lord, I just can't believe this. Why would you involve me in all this mess? You got with me for all the wrong reasons. As a matter of fact, why me? I didn't need you, I was doing just fine all by myself."

Jt looked at me and said, "Alice, I didn't know what I was doing at the time I met you, all I knew is I had to get revenge on Hattie, and whatever it took is what I was gonna do. I didn't mean to bring you into this and I definitely didn't mean you no harm. I have stayed up a many of nights thinking about this. I know when I first saw you I wanted to get with you. Yea, I did bring you into my life for the wrong reason, but it turned out to be for the right reason. Once I got to know you I fell in love with you. You are my life Alice, and I don't want to lose you. You are all I got!"

Jt was looking at me and I could feel the tears starting to run down my face. He came over to me and said, "Now Alice, as the Lord is my witness I swear I didn't mean to hurt you."

I moved back from him because I couldn't believe any of this. How could my man have been married to Hattie?

"Well Jt, what did you think would happened when I found out what you were up to? You didn't think I would find out? Our whole relationship had been nothing but a lie. Now what do you plan on doing now, killing Hattie and getting your revenge? Let me ask you one thing Jt. When I saw you for the first time outside my house that night, you had no intentions on trying to get to know me. You were just using me to get closer to Hattie? I remember when we met you was telling me you used to always see me at the Juke-Joint with another lady, you knew it was Hattie and we were friends. It all makes sense to me now."

Jt gave me and ugly smile and said, "Naw, it ain't like that."

Before he finished his sentence, I reached back and slapped him as hard as I could. It even surprised me I had slapped him so hard. I was really pissed off. I got close to his face and said, "Jt, I hate you! I can't believe you would do this to me!"

I turned to go to the bedroom but he tried to grab me by my arm. As soon as I he tried to grab me, I reached back and slapped him again. This time I slapped him harder than I did the first time.

He turned to me and said, "Listen, I ain't gonna let you keep slapping me in my face. Now that's twice, now let that be your last one."

I got even madder and said, "No you listen, you ain't letting me slap you, I am doing it on my own and you ain't gonna do a damn thing about it."

As soon as the last word came out, I slapped him right in the face again, because I knew I could get away with it. He looked at me and slapped me so hard, I stumble back into the living room.

"Dammit Alice, I just told you I ain't gonna keep letting you slap me in my face! Who in the hell do you think you are? I'm not a child!"

After I finished seeing stars, I jumped up and ran into the kitchen and pulled out one of the drawers and got me a butcher knife.

I ran back into the room and turned to Jt, "Dammit, ain't no man ever gonna put his hands on me. I'll kill him first."

He just stood there looking at me.

"Alice baby, I'm sorry. I didn't mean to hit you. I just didn't know what else to do. I didn't want you to just keep hitting me in my face. I know this is hard for you to understand. But trust me, I am telling you the truth about falling in love with you. I wanted to tell you all this early on, but I just didn't know how too. When I said, you were my life I really did mean it. I don't have any body else but you. If you forgive me, I promise you, I will never hurt you again."

He tried to take the knife out of my hand and I looked at him and knew I loved this man. He pulled on the knife again and I let go. He took it and put it back in the drawer.

I looked at Jt and said, "I still can't believe any of this. You used to be married to Hattie, I can't even picture you and her together!"

I walked into the living room and sat down in one of the chairs. I laid my head back thinking about everything. I got mad all over again.

I yelled back into the kitchen, "Shit, all this has been a lie. You ain't got to worry about Hattie killing your black ass because I'm gonna do it for her!"

Tears started to run down my face and I used the back of my sleeves to wipe the tears away. I jumped up and ran into the kitchen. I went straight to the drawer and got the knife out again, and headed for Jt. I wanted to kill him but when I got close enough; he managed to grab the knife from my hand. He pulled me close to him and tried to kiss me on my mouth. I fought him because I was mad as hell. He kept trying and wasn't letting go. His kisses started to relax me. This man knew I was weak for him. I was upset and all I ever wanted was for a man to love me for me, but it seemed he had just used me. He started to kiss me harder and I begin to relax even more, then out of nowhere he was trying to make love to me. He knew I couldn't resist his love-making. I knew he was trying to make me feel better about this, but it was gonna take a lot more than his lovemaking to make me forgive him. All of this was going through my mind while I was letting him undress me.

I didn't know what to do since I had told Alice my secret. I didn't know if I could trust her enough to tell her about what I'd done to Hattie. I knew when she got wind of Hattie being dead, she would figure out that I was behind it. I continued to hold her in my arms, kissing her on the neck while I was thinking about Hattie lying there on the side of the road in the bushes dead.

CHAPTER 42

"Hattie, Hattie, you got to come to. The doctors said, you'll be all right if you just come to but you just can't lay here in this bed, you got to fight, you got to fight for your life. You the only family I got. Lord, how can somebody do this to my sister, she ain't messing with nobody? They just go and beat her to an inch of her life and leave her for dead on the side of the road. What kind of person would do such a thing? Lord Hattie, I just got to keep on praying and not give up on you. You strong Hattie! Fight for your life!"

I looked over at Pearlie and saw the tears running down her face while she was talking to Hattie. She really did love Hattie. I couldn't help but stare at her because she was even more beautiful to me than ever. I was gonna do whatever I had to, to get her. She needed a good man in her life and I know I'm a good man.

Pearlie looked over to me and said, "Staley I don't even know if I ever thanked you for bringing my sister to the hospital. Lord knows I thank you from the bottom of my heart. If it wasn't for you, she'd be dead. She's the only family I got. I got to hold on and keep her in my prayers. I don't know who could do such a thing to her, I just don't know. I told Hattie about walking around all times of the night from that Juke-Joint all alone like she's some kind of man. Hattie ain't never been scared of anything in her life. Lord, please help her!"

I started looking around the room because I didn't know what to say. I really wanted Hattie to get better, but in the mean time I was gonna see that Pearlie didn't want or need for nothing.

I looked up and said, "Now Ms. Pearlie, I needs to get you home. It's getting late and they be putting us out of here soon anyway."

Pearlie stared at me for a long time and said, "You know what Staley, this is really the first time I have actually looked in your face? You have a really kind face. A face that haven't seen too much trouble in its life."

I didn't know what to say, so I just smiled.

She looked back down at Hattie, then back over to me, and said, "Well, all right Staley, we can go but I have to be back the first thing in the morning to check on my sister. I don't want her to think I'm not here. When she wakes up I want my face to be the first thing she sees."

Pearlie looked back down at Hattie and Hattie looked as if she was sleeping. She looked over at me and smiled.

"Look at Hattie, just resting peacefully while we all up here going crazy over her."

She put Hattie's hands in hers and closed her eyes and said a silent prayer. She sat Hattie's hands down on top of her chest and patted it, and said, "Hattie, girl, I will see you in the morning and in the meantime you try to wake up. I want to see you up and at em when I come in here in the morning, you hear me?"

I smiled, watching the way Pearlie was talking to Hattie.

On the walk home, I wanted to talk to Pearlie about trying to give me a chance to be a part of her life. I didn't know if this was a good time or not, with everything going on about her sister. We were walking and not saying anything, so I looked over to her and said, "If it's anything you need doing around the house Pearlie, just let me know and I will be right there after I get off work. Also you don't have to worry about Hattie's house none, because whatever needs doing around there, I'll be there to do it. Also don't forget, the first thing in the morning I am gonna stop by and walk you back up there to that hospital."

She looked over to me and said, "Now Staley, I know you're trying to help but you doing too much. You don't have to come over before you go to work, I can get Jimmy to walk with me. I don't want you to be all tired going to work."

I smiled and said, "Pearlie, I got all the energy I need, so just let me do what I need to do. You don't have to worry about me none, you got your sister to worry about right now."

We both started laughing and I felt as if we were getting closer. After that, neither one of us said anything. We both just walked and smiled.

I reached over and grabbed Pearlie's hand and said, "I don't want nobody to steal you while we're out here walking on this dark road."

She started to pull her hand back, but she didn't. She just kept her hand in mine. "It's been a long time since I've had the company of a man, and I feel peaceful about my life. I guess by Hattie being in the hospital it makes me realize I have to start living my life."

I started telling her everything would be all right with Hattie, the Lord will work it out.

We got to the house and I walked her up on the porch. Pearlie turned towards the door and said, "Now I don't know how many times I have to tell that boy to leave the porch light on. It's just too dark out here, anybody could come here and get him."

I turned Pearlie around to face me and said, "Pearlie, thank you for letting me walk you home, it was a nice walk. Now don't forget, I'll be by here the first thing in the morning to walk you up there to the hospital. Don't you leave fore I get here."

She looked at me and said, "Now Staley, I told you that you don't have to go through all the trouble of getting up early. Jimmy is here and he can walk with me."

I pulled her in closer to me and put my arms around her waist and said, "Now we just talked about it and I am gonna do this. I'll see you in the morning, and I don't want to hear nothing else about it, okay?"

I had gotten so close I could smell the sweetness of her scent. I didn't want to let her go. She pulled back out of my arms and opened the screen door and stopped and turned around as if she wanted to say something. I looked at her wondering what it was she wanted to say. I stood there but she didn't say anything. She just turned, opened the door and walked inside the house.

I stood on the porch wondering what had just happened. I started walking down the steps and turned around and saw Pearlie peeping out the curtains. I waved at her and she waved back. She continued to watch me out the window. Every time I would take a few steps, I would turn around to see if she was still watching me. She continued to do this until I had walked down the road into the darkness. I knew she couldn't see me anymore, because I couldn't see her in the window.

CHAPTER 43

❀

I got up the next morning thinking about everything Jt had told me about Hattie. I was thinking about it all through the night. Every time I rolled over, I could see Hattie face. I still couldn't believe they used to be married. This was all too strange for me. I hadn't seen Hattie in awhile, but I heard she had changed a lot since BoHenry had passed on. People who stopped by to check on her said she seemed to be all into herself. She was kinda walking around in a daze. She wasn't messing with anybody and didn't talk a lot of trash like she used too, as a matter of fact it seemed like she was trying to mellow out. I thought about all the mess that Hattie had caused and started to laugh. It would be a cold day in hell before Hattie mellowed out.

I started remembering my times with Hattie. I felt that over all she had been a good friend. She had always been there when I needed her. Back in my mind I knew I still had plans for Hattie.

I couldn't picture Hattie and Jt together. I was still trying to make two plus two on this. I wondered why Hattie didn't say anything to me when I told her Jt's name. She knew who he was since she had been married to him. A lot of this wasn't making sense to me. I loved Jt, but I didn't want anything to happened to Hattie. I didn't know what to do, but I knew I needed to talk to Hattie.

The next morning Jt left early for work. This would give me more time to think of a much needed plan. I had to warn Hattie about what Jt planned on doing to her. Lord what am I gonna do about this? This burden is just too much to carry.

I sat down in the living room so I could get my thinking right. Everything was running through my mind. The first thing I needed to do was to get dress and go on over to Hattie's. I knew things would fall into place once I talked to her. She would explain it all to me. I would tell her everything about him. About who he says he was and everything he planned on doing to her. I wondered what Jt would do to me once he found out I told Hattie everything about him. Suppose if Jt and Hattie were in this together and they're trying to set me up? I was so confused.

After I got dressed, I went back into the living room and sat on the chair thinking.

"Lord what should I do? Suppose if Hattie was only pretending to be my friend, and set me up with Jt to hurt me, or suppose if everything Jt said about Hattie was true and he was planning on killing her, then what?"

My head started hurting trying to make sense out of this. I started on my way down to the Bottom. I stepped out on the porch and looked up towards the sun.

"Lord this sun is sho nuff hot today."

I had no ideal how I was gonna get to the Bottom so I started walking when a car pulled over. I looked inside and it was an older man and what looked to be his wife. He asked me, "Do you need a ride, where are you going?"

I told him I was headed to the Bottom. They told me to get in, that they were going that way. When I finally got to the Bottom I was a little upset because all the while I was sitting in the car, the old man kept looking back in his mirror winking his old eye at me. Now he knew he shouldn't be doing that. He was just a disrespectful old man.

When they let me out the car I started walking over to Hattie's. I got to the house and knocked on the door and noticed no one was there. It felt kinda strange because Hattie or somebody is always there. I didn't know what to do. I really needed to talk to Hattie and I wasn't going back home until I got to the bottom of Jt's story. I needed to find out what Hattie knew, and to get some answers. After getting tired of knocking, I walked off the porch and looked around to see which direction I was gonna go in. I had no ideal where to look for Hattie, so I decided to see if she was at the Juke-Joint. I walked all the way up there in the hot sun. When I got there the place was locked down. Something just didn't seem right. I couldn't figure out where Hattie would be at this time of the day. It wasn't like she could get lost in this little town. I knew somebody knew where Hattie was. I thought about going down to Pearlie, but Lord I just can't keep walking out here in this hot sun. I'm gonna mess around and have a heat stroke.

I started down to Pearlie's and walked on the porch. The screen door was opened. I put my face up to the screen to look inside to see if I could see anybody moving, but the house was still. I yelled through the screen door, "Pearlie! Pearlie, are you in there?"

I could see Pearlie coming out from one of the back room, coming towards the door. She looked surprise to see me standing there. She opened the screen door and said, "Alice is that you, what in the world are you doing here? I can't believe you are out here walking in this hot sun, Girl, what don got into you?"

She looked me up and down and said, "Lord girl you sweating like it's raining outside. Come on in here so I can get you a cold glass of lemonade to cool you off."

I walked inside and sat on the sofa and said, "Now Pearlie that sho would be kind of you, but I don't have much time, I am looking for your sista. It's mighty important that I talk to her."

Pearlie stopped and turned around and looked at me and said, "Haven't you heard?"

I looked up and said, "Heard what?"

"Hold on one second while I get you something to drink, then we can talk."

Pearlie started off into the kitchen leaving me alone in the living room. I sat there on the sofa looking around noticing how clean and in place everything seemed. I smiled when I saw a picture of Pearlie, Jimmy and some man I had never seen before. I figured it must be a picture of Pearlie's husband. I knew the picture was taken a long time ago, seeing how big Jimmy is now. I looked around and saw a picture of Hattie and Pearlie as little girls with their mother and father. I was thinking to myself, "Hattie has always been ugly, even as a child."

I started to laugh to myself. I picked up the picture to get a closer look. I said in a light whisper, "They sho nuff don't look nuthin alike."

I started to look around at the other pictures that were sitting up on the mantelpiece, when Pearlie came back into the living room. She walked over to me and said, "I made you some fresh lemonade so we can talk."

I looked at Pearlie and said, "You got some old pictures up there."

Pearlie turned around and looked back at the pictures and started to smile.

"Time just seems to get away from you. Just seems like yesterday those pictures were taken."

I started back to the sofa and sat down and said, "Now tell me what it is about Hattie I haven't heard."

Pearlie sat down in the chair facing me and said, "Baby, Hattie is in the hospital. Somebody tried to beat her to death, within an inch of her life, and left her on the side of the road in some bushes halfway dead."

I was looking at Pearlie's lip moving but I didn't hear anything else after she said somebody had tried to kill Hattie. All I could think about is what Jt had said he was gonna do to her. The more Pearlie's lip moved, the more I thought about it and knew Jt had done this to Hattie. That is exactly what he told me he was gonna do. I just sat there in a daze until Pearlie grabbed my hands and said, "Baby, she's gonna be just fine. The doctors up there said she gonna be alright because she's strong and a fighter."

I hadn't even notice or felt the tears running down my face. I looked up at Pearlie and asked, "How and when did this happened?"

"Baby I'm just surprised you haven't heard anything about it. Everybody around town has been talking about it. It happened over the weekend, late Saturday night, early Sunday morning."

I held my head down and said, "Does anybody know who did this?"

"Naw, ain't nobody said nothing yet. I have told Hattie so many times about walkin home after work in the dark from that place."

I couldn't take it no more and said, "Well who found her?"

"Do you know Staley, BoHenry's brother? Well he's staying with Hattie for a spell. He's the one who found her. He noticed she hadn't come home that night and went to look for her. When he was on his way up to that Devil's place, he found her laying out by the side of the road like some animal."

Pearlie looked up at the ceiling and said, "Lord, I've always said that place was nuthin but the devil's play ground."

She continued talking, "While Staley was walkin, he found her there on the side of the road in some bushes bout halfway dead. I went up there to the hospital, and Lord knows I didn't even recognize my own sista, that's how bad she had been beaten. She was beaten within an inch of her life. Lord knows if it wasn't for Staley, she would surely be dead. He's a good man and Lord, I thank you for him."

I just sat there, knowing all of this was Jt's doing. I didn't know how to tell Pearlie what I knew. I didn't know what to do knowing all of this. I couldn't believe this. This was just too much for me right now. I had to talk to Jt. I needed to hear it from his own mouth that he had done this.

CHAPTER 44

After hearing everything Pearlie was saying about Hattie, I decided to leave and go straight to the hospital. When I got there, I opened the door to Hattie's room and Jimmy was sitting on the edge of the bed holding Hattie's hand. He turned around to see who was coming into the room. When he saw me, a smile came to his face. He seemed happy to see me. I looked at him and he looked as if he had been crying. I walked over to him and gave him a kiss on the head.

"It's been a long time since I last saw you. You have really grown up. You're nearly a man now."

Jimmy started to smile and said, "Thank you Ms. Alice."

I looked down at Hattie and didn't even recognize her. I just busted out crying. "How could Jt have done something like this?"

I grabbed her hand and held it in mine and said, "Hattie it's gonna be all right, just keep fighting and getting better."

I looked over to Jimmy and asked, "How's Hattie holding up?"

Jimmy looked over at Hattie and then back at me.

"I guess she knows we're here. She can't talk much but she keeps mumbling something."

Jimmy looked up to me and said, "Ms. Alice, I'm glad you're here. Maybe you can understand what she's tryin to say."

I bent down over Hattie and put my ear to her mouth trying to hear something, but she wasn't saying anything. The longer I stayed down there I could feel the tears starting to form in my eyes. I looked back up to Jimmy and ask him to let me have some time alone with Hattie. He got up and headed for the door, saying he was going downstairs. When he was leaving out, I stopped him and asked him where was his mama?

He turned back and said, "She said she was going to take care of some business and for me to stay here with A_nt Hattie till she gets back."

"All right then, go head on downstairs."

When the door closed, I looked down into Hattie's face and started telling her everything I knew about Jt. Who he was and how he was gonna try to kill her. I didn't know if she could hear me or not, but I had to tell her what I knew. I had to get it off my mind before I went crazy. While I was talking I could hear Hattie mumbling something. I put my ear to her mouth and it sounded something like, "Mosiah."

I leaned down closer and it sounded like the word, "Josiah."

I had no ideal what Hattie was tryin to say. All of a sudden Jimmy walked in and sat down on the side of the bed in a chair. Hattie mumble again, "Josiah."

I looked over to Jimmy and told him to let me have some more time with Hattie and I would come and get him when I was finished. This was grown folks stuff and he didn't need to bother himself with it.

I tried to ask Hattie what was a Josiah? She never said, she just kept saying it over and over again.

I went downstairs for Jimmy and he came back upstairs with me. Once he sat down I asked him, "Have you ever heard Hattie mention what a Josiah or Mosiah was? I have no ideal what Hattie is trying to say."

He start telling me that Hattie used to be married to a man named Josiah before she met Uncle Bo.

While I was looking down at Hattie, I started thinking about Jt being married to her and still couldn't see it. I wondered if his real name was Josiah. Now all this time I had spent with him, I have never known what his real name was.

I continued talking to Hattie telling her everything I knew. I felt nothing but pain, knowing the man I had fell in love with could commit such a horrible act.

Jimmy was listening to everything I was saying. He held his head up and said, "Ms. Alice, I can't understand why somebody would do something like this to A_nt Hattie."

Jimmy started to tell me he had heard A_nt Hattie talk about a man name Josiah before and thought he was dead. He remembered the first day she came back to Topeka, and told his mama about how she killed her husband, Josiah. Apparently she didn't kill him good enough.

I sat there all day holding Hattie's hand. She kept going in and out of consciousness. Lord, I hope she gonna be all right. I tried to talk to her when she was awake, but right in the middle of my conversation she would fall into a deep sleep.

When I got home late that night, Jt was sitting in the living room. I spoke to him, but he didn't say anything.

I asked him, "What you doing home so early?"

He still didn't say anything. I stopped dead in my tracks and said; "Now I know you hear me talking to you. You got something on your mind, or the cat don got your tongue?"

He stood up and said, "Alice, where have you been all day?"

I turned around and said, "Ain't been nowhere, why you ask me that?"

Jt got out of the chair and walked over to me and said, "I came home early today and you haven't been here since I've been here, and I've been here over four hours. Now you want to tell me where you've been?"

"Well Jt, I had some running around to do."

"Alice, what type of running around did you do? I don't see any grocery, so you didn't go to the grocery store. Don't see any shopping bags, so you didn't go shopping, now you want to tell me what type of running around you been doing?"

I stood there looking at Jt, not knowing what to say. I hadn't planned on him being home so early and hadn't thought of a plan or a lie to tell him. So I didn't say anything.

He came closer and grabbed me by the arm and turned me around facing him. "Don't you hear me talking to you!"

I looked into Jt's face and had never seen him this mad before. I didn't know what to say or if I should say anything at all. He started yelling, "I know you went looking for Hattie to tell her about what I was gonna do to her. Now didn't you?"

He still had me by my arm. I looked up at him and still didn't say anything. He looked me straight in the eyes and said, "I ain't gonna keep asking ask. Now where in the hell have you been?"

I didn't know what to say but I knew I had to say something.

"Somebody told me that Hattie was found halfway dead on the side of the road. Not to far from the Juke-Joint. Is that your doing, Jt?"

Jt got madder and said, "Alice, you don't ask me any questions till you tell me where you've been."

I snatched my arm out of Jt's hand and yelled out, "Yea, I went to find Hattie to tell her about what you were gonna do, but I guess I got there too late? I know you probably thought that you killed her but you didn't. I heard you messed her up pretty good tho. I went up to the hospital to see about her."

I got closer and said, "Jt, I looked at Hattie in that bed and didn't even recognize her. If you did it, you beat her within an inch of her life."

He looked at me with hatred in his eyes. He didn't say anything. He just stared at me and turned around and walked out the door. He slammed the door so hard, he nearly took the hinges off the door. My heart was beating so fast I had to sit down. I knew he was gonna do the same thing to me that he done to Hattie. Lord, I have to watch my steps now.

About a week had passed and Jt hadn't come home since we had our fight. I didn't know what to do. I didn't know what he was planning on doing. I asked around about him, but nobody knew where he was. A lot of people didn't even know who he was. They were looking at me like I was crazy when I was trying to describe how he looked. I hoped he hadn't done anything to himself. I realized after he had been gone, that I really loved and missed him. Since the day we met we have never missed a day being together. Now my man had been gone for more than a week. I didn't know what to do about Jt hurting Hattie. I just didn't know. Then I started thinking that he never did say anything about tryin to kill Hattie. Maybe he didn't do it after all. Hattie has a lot of enemies out there.

My heart was aching, and it wouldn't let me think clear. I missed Jt and I wanted him back home.

CHAPTER 45

Two weeks had passed and I still hadn't heard anything from Jt. Nobody had seen him or heard from him. I was really worried about him now. I realized how much I loved him and I would do whatever it takes to get him back.

I went back to the hospital to check on Hattie. I walked into the room and Pearlie and a man were standing by the window. Pearlie turned around and saw me coming through the door and smiled. I walked over to Pearlie and hugged her for a long time. Pearlie backed away and looked over and said, "Alice, this is Staley and Staley this is Alice."

He smiled while he was looking at me. "Please to meet ya."

Pearlie glanced over at him and gave him a dirty look. Pearlie turned back toward me and said, "Alice, this is Staley, BoHenry's brother."

I gave him my hand and said, "Glad to meet you again. Sorry to hear about your brother. He was a good friend of mine."

I turned around to Pearlie and asked, "How is Hattie holding up this evening?"

Pearlie turned toward Hattie and looked down at her and said, "I think she's gonna make it, look at her she has improved a bit. Hopefully she'll get better and we can take her home soon."

I looked down at Hattie. She was starting to look a little like her old self again. I didn't want to wake her but I did need to talk to her.

I looked over at Pearlie and asked, "Pearlie do you mind if I could talk to you for a minute in private?"

Pearlie looked over at Staley and said, "Ill be back in a minute. If you need me I'll just be down the hall."

We left the room and walked down the hall and sat in some chairs on the side of the wall. I looked up and down the hall and pushed two chairs together so we could talk. I started talking to Pearlie telling her everything I knew about Jt. She was looking at me in shock knowing Josiah had been in town all this time and he was the one who put Hattie in the hospital. She looked at me and said, "Hattie told me she had killed Josiah. Lord, what in the world is going on?"

While I was talking, she kept looking directly at me. She put her hands up to her mouth like I was telling her a secret.

"Alice, I can't believe this! That man has been living here all along and nobody knew about it? How can this be! I guess he came here for revenge on Hattie, huh? I think he got the best of her too."

She turned and looked down the hall then back at me and said, "You know Alice, I have been telling Hattie for as long as I can remember that she should turn over her soul. That's a saying my Aunt Mable used to say to us all the time. You know Hattie is something else. She can't keep being mean to people and expect to get away with it. She has ten lives. I guess she ain't gonna leave this earth, until the good Lord says so, tho. I just can't get over Josiah being right here in Topeka and trying to kill Hattie."

Pearlie stood up and said, "Well where is Josiah now?"

"I haven't seen him in about two weeks, Pearlie. I have no ideal where he is."

Pearlie looked confused and said, "Well you have to go to the police and tell them what you know. Hopefully they'll try to do something about this mess."

"Now Pearlie you know they ain't gonna do much since we black. They don't care about us unless we trying to kill one of them."

"Lord, that ain't nuthin but the truth Alice. Been that way all my life since I've been living here. It's a shame how they treat us."

"Alice, I just don't know what to do. I can't let Josiah keep trying to kill my sista. I got to do something. I know if I talked to him, I could talk some sense into him."

I reached over and held her hand because I knew she was getting upset.

"Well Pearlie I ain't seen the man in about two weeks. I don't even know if he's dead or alive."

We continued talking when Staley came out the room calling for Pearlie. He started telling her that Hattie was trying to wake up. We both rushed down the hall and back into the room. We went to Hattie's bedside and she had her eyes opened. Tears were running down the side of her face. She looked over to me and said, "Alice, you're the last person I expected to see here."

Hattie tried to smile but I could see it was painful for her. She held up her hand for me to hold. I held her hand and she started telling me she heard everything I was saying about Jt. She started telling me that she didn't even know Josiah was still alive. She tried to raise her head and said, "I thought I had killed him, but I guess I didn't do a good job huh?"

We all started to laugh. I turned toward Hattie and said, "Girl I am sho glad you're getting better. I'm glad you are awake. You really gave us a scare. When I first came up here I couldn't even tell if I had the right room. That's how bad you looked."

Hattie started to smile and said, "Girl, did I look that bad?"

I laughed and said, "Well you ain't never really been pretty, so you know if I didn't recognize you, then you know you musta looked pretty bad."

We all started to laugh, when Hattie yelled out, "Now ya'll know I can't be laughin, ya'll gonna make me break my stitches. After Hattie stopped laughing, she looked over to Pearlie and said, "Pearlie baby, can you give me some time to talk to Alice for a minute? We needs to be alone. Y'all just leave out the room, this won't take but a minute."

Everybody left out the room. Hattie still had hold of my hand. I looked down at her and she looked as if she had fallen asleep. Then all of a sudden she took a deep breath and said, "Alice I heard you talkin to me when I was sick and I know about Josiah. He's the one who put me here in this hospital. I know he thinks I'm dead, but the Lord has other plans for me besides his. I guess I'm reapin what I've sow."

I looked down and ask, "Hattie, what we gonna do about Josiah? Everything is just a mess. He was living with me and he used to be married to you?"

She turned her head sideways and just stared at the wall. Then she turned back and stared at me.

"I guess I was just dumb and didn't put two and two together. Even when you told me your mans name I didn't figure it out. His real name is Josiah Ray Thompson. Yeap, that's exactly what it is. Lord, where he gets Jt from I'll never know. I thought that man was dead!"

She let go of my hand and a tear had started to fall down her face. She wiped the tear from her eye.

"Alice, when I was out of my mind all I could think about was the people who loved me. As a matter of fact, I went back a long way thinkin about all my kin, you, Lonnie, Aunt Mable, Pearlie, BoHenry, just everybody. I even thought about Josiah from time to time. I was thinking bout my life. I know I've got to make some changes."

Tears started to run down her face. She turned her head sideways, closing her eyes. She stayed that way for a while. I just stood there holding her hand. I didn't know what Hattie was going through. I felt sorry for her. She was in more pain than just from her beating.

She turned back around and looked straight at me. Then she placed her other hand on top of my mine.

"Alice, I want to see Josiah and talk to him cause we even now. Can't hold no madness against him cause I was wrong. I have to make everything right again. I tried to kill him and I know I really hurt him. So Alice if you see him, tell him he didn't kill me, he came close but he didn't, and I want to talk to him. I needs to ask him for his forgiveness. Ain't gonna press charges on him either. Just ain't gonna do it. I want to make everything right."

After she said that she seemed happier. I guess she felt she was doing the right thing. She raised up a little bit and said, "Alice, gon on out there and get my family. Tell them to come on in now. I needs to see em.

Jimmy came straight to the bed smiling. He leaned over and hugged Hattie. He whispered something into her ear, and she started smiling. She rubbed him on his back and said, "Jimmy, gon and get me some water. Been talking too much and my throat don got dry. I'm gonna be alright boy. Ole Hattie ain't goin nowhere no time soon. Yeap, I'm gonna be alright."

Jimmy came back with the water and Hattie drank all of it. She looked up at Pearlie and reached for her hand. She held Pearlie's hand and said, "Thank God for you Pearlie, you the only family I got. We have to look out for each other. I got some serious changes to make in my life."

I looked over at Pearlie and then back at Hattie and notice Hattie had fallen asleep. Pearlie looked down at Hattie and said, "Alice, Hattie gonna be all right. I guess she's tryin to heal her soul along with her scars. She used to be meaner than a snake, now she's tryin to turn over her soul. It took all this to finally make her, but thank God she's trying to do it."

I smiled and felt good about Hattie. I looked over to Pearlie and said, "Well yea, it looks like things are gonna be all right. I guess I'll come up here later in the week to check on her. Do you know when she supposed to be getting out?"

Pearlie looked down at Hattie and then back up to me.

"The doctors said I can take her home by the end of next week if she keeps improving. She looks like she doing pretty good to me."

I looked over at Pearlie and smiled, "If she's not here when I come back next week, then I know she's home. Try to get word to me to let me know when she leaving out of here, all right? Do you know if she's gonna be stayin with you or at her own house?"

Pearlie smiled and said, "I know I'm gonna have to fight Hattie but she's comin home with me till she can do for herself. I know she got Staley there, but she needs to be with family. Got to make sure she gets backs to her old self. Get all her strength back fore I let her back out into the world. Lord, I'm glad she gonna make it."

CHAPTER 46

✥

I was glad that Hattie was getting better, and out of the hospital. During my walk home from the hospital I started thinking about Jt. Wondering where in the world could he be and why he hasn't come home yet? Lord, I hope that man is alright!

I walked into the house and to my surprise, Jt was sitting at the kitchen table. I was really happy to see him. That man didn't know how much I've missed him. I wanted to run right up to him and hug him, but no I was mad. Seeing him and knowing that he was all right was all I needed. I looked at him and he had his face down in his hands. I stopped and looked at him again. On one hand I was glad to see him, and on the other I couldn't believe what he had done to Hattie. I knew in my heart he had done this, but I was gonna listen to whatever he had to say. Jt raised his head up and looked at me. I noticed his eyes were bloodshot. He got up from the table and came toward me. He was stumbling around and I knew he was good and drunk. He got close to me and I could smell alcohol on his breathe. I thought he was coming up on me to hug me. I walked up on him and all of a sudden he slapped me in the face with the back of his hand. I grabbed my face and stumble backward. He approached me again and I backed up. I didn't know what in the world was going on. He hadn't said a word not even a hello. He came toward me again so fast I couldn't move out the way and with all his might he slapped me again as hard as he could. I fell to the floor. I was in a daze.

I started yelling, "Jt, what the hell don got into you! Why are you beating on me?"

He approached me again. I got up from the floor and started to run through the house. He started running behind me. When he got closer to me, I knew he was gonna hit me again, so I ran out the back door. I knew he was too drunk to come out here or to get down the steps.

Jt started yelling something about me telling his business and he couldn't trust me. I couldn't understand what he was saying because my face was still burning and I could feel his handprint on my face. I was looking around for someplace to hide. I thought about running around to the front door, but I had locked it when I came inside.

Jt pushed opened the back screen door so hard it slammed against the house. I ran toward the shed and watched him come out the back door stumbling down the steps.

When he got to the bottom step he fell to the ground. I knew he was good and drunk. He looked in my direction and yelled, "Come here heffa, you come here now!"

He got up and stumbled around. I tried to stay hidden and quiet so he wouldn't see me.

He started yelling, "You ain't nuthin but a hussy, I said come on over here, I can see you!"

I looked around to see how I could get away from Jt if he started coming in my direction.

I yelled back, "Jt, now you're drunk, gon back into the house and sleep it off. Go and lay down. I'll come and lay down with you if you want me too, okay?"

He started coming towards me. I didn't think he could see me. I looked at him stumbling around and thought he looked kinda funny. He came right over to the shed and I ran inside. He came inside after me. There wasn't much room to run or hide. He saw me and tried to lunge at me. He almost grabbed me, but I moved back. I moved around him to get out the shed. I was gonna lock him inside but when I got to the door, I noticed there wasn't a lock on it. I turned around to look for a rope or something to hold the door. I had my body up against it when all of a sudden Jt busted through the door and knocked it opened. He hit the door so hard it knocked me back. I stumbled over something and fell to the ground. He saw me lying there and came up on me. He reached out and tried to grab me by the leg. I started kicking and rolling around, but he got the bottom of my pant leg and started pulling me. I couldn't believe he was this strong, while he was drunk. He pulled me closer enough to him to grab my shirt. He pulled me right up to his face where we were eye to eye. I closed my eyes because I knew he was gonna hit me. Then all of a sudden he slammed me right into the ground. When I hit the ground I thought I was gonna pass out. I knew something was broken inside my body.

He grabbed me by the back of my hair and just started punching me in my back. This fool was fighting me like I was a man. I started screaming, feeling the pain running all through my body. I tried to get away, but the pain was too bad. I got up on my knees and tried to crawl into the shed. I knew once I got in there, I could hide somewhere, anywhere. I just knew I had to get away. I got into the shed, and looked around. I didn't know he was walking right behind me. He pulled me up off the ground by my hair again and turned me toward him and hit me in the face with his fist nearly knocking me unconscious. I was trying to fight him back, but he was stronger than I thought. I knew he was gonna kill me if I didn't get away from him. I was fighting back as hard as I could. I thought about trying to get back inside the house. I had to get the gun. I was gonna kill him. He grabbed me up off the ground by my hair again. I was starting to black out, when I remember something my mama always told me.

"Any time a man got you in a situation you can't get yourself out of, go for his private parts."

I reached back with all my might, and hit that man so hard in his private parts, he bent over holding himself and fell to the ground. I tried to get away, but all of a sudden he stood back up like it didn't even faze him. I couldn't believe this!

He yelled out, "So you tryin to ruin me, huh! He grabbed me again and hit me in the face. I felt my mouth filling up with blood. I knew I couldn't take too much more of this. I fell to the ground holding my head. He started kicking me in my side and back. I balled up in a knot so the kicks wouldn't hurt so much. I just laid there in a daze tryin to catch my breath. Every time he would kick me the pain would go through my entire body. I knew I was dying. I just laid there praying, asking the Lord to forgive all my sins, when all of a sudden I hear this loud voice. I looked over towards the shed door and I could see a blur of a shadow. It was definitely a man. Was my mind playing tricks on me? Was Jt kicking me that hard?

All of a sudden I see this shadow coming towards Jt. The shadow stopped and picked something up off the ground. It looked like a shovel. He started swinging it and hit Jt so hard knocking him off of me. Jt turned around and looked up. He got up and started fighting toward the shadow. Jt charged at him and the shadow moved sideways. They both started fighting. The shadow broke loose from Jt and swung again with the shovel hitting Jt on his side.

I just laid there on the ground. I could hear them arguing, but I couldn't make out what was being said. My head and body were hurting so bad. I couldn't keep my eyes open to see what was going on. The shadow sounded like he was saying something about, "Tryin to kill Hattie," but with the ringing in my ears, I just couldn't understand what they were saying.

I opened my eyes and the shadow was swinging the shovel again. Jt grabbed the shovel. They hung onto it fighting, trying to get it loose from the other. They were going around and around and fell to the ground. They wrestled around on the ground, and I tried to watch them, but my neck wouldn't move. Then all of a sudden they both got up. As soon as the shadow got up, he hit Jt in the face with his fist, making him lose his grip on the shovel. I tried to get up and move out the way but my head and body wouldn't move. I tried again with all my might, but I just couldn't move.

The shadow moved in closer and hit Jt over the head with the shovel or whatever it was he had. I looked at the shadow again trying to figure out who this was. I tried to keep my eyes open, but they were burning like somebody had put pepper in them. Everything was just a blurred. I tried to watch, when all of a sudden Jt felled backward to the ground, landing at the bottom of my legs. The shadow dived on top of him and they both wrestle around. Jt kicked the shadow off him and they both stood up yelling at each other. I still couldn't understand what they were saying. All of a sudden Jt hit the shadow knocking him to the ground. He fell on my leg. I kicked him off me. The shadow got up and charged Jt by grabbing him under his legs and picked him up and slammed him right into the ground. The shadow went over to Jt and looked down at him. Jt wasn't moving. He picked up the shovel and started hitting Jt everywhere, like he was a mad man. The shadow was going crazy!

I started yelling to the shadow, "Stop! Please stop! If you keep hitting him like that you're gonna kill him. Please don't kill him! I love him!" The shadow continued beating him.

I could barely move my body. I turned on my side to look at Jt and blood was everywhere! He was so bloody, I had to turn my head away. I couldn't stand to see my man laying there in all that blood not knowing if he was dead or alive. The shadow stopped beating him and looked down at him again. He was out of breath, and was breathing hard. He looked over to me and said, "Everything gonna be all right."

The shadow started looking around the shed. Then all of a sudden he went to the other side of the shed and pulled that plastic back from over the hole. He grabbed Jt by the legs and drugged him over to the hole and pushed him into it. When Jt landed in the hole, I heard a grunt. The shadow took the shovel and start throwing dirt over him.

I couldn't believe what I was seeing! How could somebody do this to my Jt? I loved him and didn't want to be without him. I couldn't take this anymore. I had to stop him. I tried to move, but my body was paralyzed.

Why is he throwing dirt over him and he isn't even dead? Didn't he hear him make that noise? What in the world is he doing?

I yelled out, "He ain't dead! Why you doing this? You gonna kill him! Don't do that! I was saying some of anything to get him to stop covering Jt up with that dirt. I had tired myself out and needed to rest. I needed to get to the house to get the police and get my gun. I kept trying to say something to the shadow to stop him from doing this, but my mouth was sore and no words would come out. I felt like I was gonna pass out. I tried with all my might, but nothing happened. I just gave up and closed my eyes and laid there. I laid there and started getting comfortable when all of a sudden I could feel myself being lifted and carried out. I knew I was being taken out of the shed, because I could feel the light on my face. I was hurting all over my entire body. I just needed to rest and wake up from this terrible dream. While I was being carried, I tried to look at the shadow to see if I could make out who this was. I tried to open my eyes, but the sunlight was burning them. All I could see was a blur and darkness. When we got into the house, I felt the shadow laying me down on the couch. I didn't have a clue to who this was. I didn't want to open my eyes anymore. I felt better; knowing this was all over, all I needed was some rest, and to wake up from this terrible dream.

CHAPTER 47

I didn't know what day it was when I woke up on the couch. I started thinking about the dream I had. I looked down on the floor, and saw a pan of water with a washcloth in it. The water was bloody. I looked around the room thinking somebody else was in the house besides me, so I called out, "Jt, Jt," but no one answered. I tried to move but I was too sore. I was lying there on the couch with my hands up to my face and could feel a bandage wrapped around my head. I patted the bandage and said out loud, "Lord, please tell me this was nothing but a dream."

I called out again, "Jt, Jt!"

I knew within my soul it wasn't a dream because I was too sore. I was trying hard to remember what happened, but none of it made sense to me. I remember coming home and seeing Jt and him hitting me in the face. We were fighting in the shed and somebody knocked him off me. Was he tryin to kill me? Who was it that knocked him off me? Did somebody cover Jt up in that hole in the shed? Naw, that can't be!

I tried to get off the couch but my body was too sore. I tried harder but I couldn't get up. I was just lying there thinking about everything that happened that day and fell into a really deep sleep.

The next day I woke up I was still on the couch. I couldn't move a muscle. I was so sore I couldn't even turn my body over. My mouth had swollen to the point where it was hard for me to swallow. I put my hands up to my face and could feel my eyes were swollen as well. I looked down on the floor and the same pan full of bloody water was still there. I thought about the dream I had, about Jt being thrown in the hole in the shed. With all my might I tried to pull myself up from the couch. I needed to get up from here. I was lying there looking up at the ceiling, thinking about everything and started to cry. The tears were burning my eyes. I didn't know what to do. I tried again with all my might, and hollered out, "Lord please help me!"

It was all too much for me so I just laid there thinking about my life.

Days passed and I laid on the couch until I couldn't take it any more. I knew I had to get up. It took everything in me to manage to sit up and put my feet on the floor. I just wanted to sit there for a minute and get myself together. I sat there running my hands through my hair trying to make some sense out of this. I pushed up off the couch and stumbled over to the mirror. I looked into the mirror and didn't even recognize myself. I said out loud, "Oh my God! I looked like somebody was trying to kill me."

I thought about Jt again and knew I needed to get down to the shed. I had to see for myself if I was dreaming. I tried to move around but I was hurting so bad. I went over to the couch and sat back down and started crying. I needed to see for myself what had really happened in the shed. I laid back on the couch when I felt the tears running down my face. I looked out towards the window and saw the sun setting. I was gonna lay here until in the morning and hopefully I would feel better.

The first thing the next morning, I realized I felt a little better. I tried to get up off the couch. It took everything I had, but I finally got up and stumble around feeling like I was just learning to walk. I made it over to the kitchen and looked out the window towards the shed. It was really quiet down there and nothing looked like it was out of the place. I noticed the door to the shed was lying on the ground.

I started back into the living room and sat back down on the chair. This was too heavy on my mind. I sat there trying to replay everything in my mind. None of it made sense. I started to cry. My side was killing me. I couldn't help it but the tears started to flow, and it was a much-needed cry. The tears started burning my eyes. I laid down and fell asleep.

When I woke up, the first thing on my mind was going down to the shed. I needed to put some closure on what happened. I had to see for myself. I got up and thanked God I didn't hurt so bad. I made it to the kitchen and looked out at the shed. I went to the backdoor and opened it and walked down the steps taking it one step at a time. With each and every step I took, I was holding onto my side. The sun was shining so bright that I had to squint my eyes to see. I couldn't even walk straight being in so much pain. I staggered towards the shed and when I got to the doorway, my heart started racing. I stood there and couldn't move. I looked around. My heart was beating so fast, I thought it was gonna come right out of my chest. I knew I couldn't take it and was gonna pass out. With all my strength I walked inside to where the plastic was. I stood there looking down. I didn't know if I wanted to know or not. I didn't know what to do. I took a few steps back because I decided I didn't want to know after all. I was just gonna let it go and head on back up to the house. I knew I couldn't do that because it would haunt me for the rest of my life.

I moved a few steps up and bent down and snatched the plastic back and looked down. The hole had been covered up. I just stood there not moving. When it hit me, I fell down to my knees, crying, shaking, and trembling, knowing Jt was under that dirt. I thought about the shadow and couldn't understand how he could bury a man alive. I yelled out! "Lord why? Who could be that mean?" I just stay there yelling and crying.

I got off my knees in a daze. I didn't know what I was gonna do. I thought about getting a shovel and seeing if Jt was buried there. I had to get myself together. I started crying while turning around walking back up to the house. My knees were weak. All types of thoughts were running through my head. I knew I had to go to the police.

CHAPTER 48

For the next couple of months, I mostly stayed to myself, going to visit Hattie every once in awhile. I couldn't understand what had happened in my life or how it could get turned upside down so fast. I couldn't accept the fact that Jt was killed and was no longer a part of my life. It was hard for me because I saw it all happened with my own eyes and I couldn't figure out who did it, or why? I went to the police to explain every thing to them and they looked at me as if I was crazy. They wouldn't even come out to the shed so I could show them where the body was buried. I thought about digging the body up myself, to prove to my mind I wasn't going crazy. I knew I couldn't stay in that house any longer. It had too many bad memories attached to it. I had to move back into town. There was no reason for me to be out here by myself anyway.

Once I moved back into town, everything seemed different. After going through that experience, I knew I wasn't the same person I used to be. When I was out and about, I looked at everybody's face I passed, to see if they showed any signs or said anything that would give me a clue as to who killed Jt. I wanted to find out who killed him and why?

Time passed and Hattie got out of the hospital and was staying with Pearlie until she could get on her feet. She was getting ready to move back in her own house soon. Everybody was talking about how much she had changed, and how much better she looked.

When I was moving out that house, I hated going in and out of there, knowing somebody had killed Jt in the back shed. I just didn't know what I was gonna do. I didn't know if I should tell somebody else about what happened. After I tried to explain it to the police and heard how it sounded and saw the way they looked at me, I knew I couldn't keep telling that story.

Months passed and I tried to get on with my life. I was lonely and alone. I didn't have any directions. I knew I didn't want to go to the Juke-Joint anymore. I didn't want that part of my life anymore. I still wanted a good man, a man I could grow old with and have as good company. I had learned my lessons and I wouldn't settle for just any man. My life had taken a turn in a different direction. I started going to church and really putting my life into learning the Lord. I had so much hatred in my heart. I knew the only way to find peace was to give my life over to him, or as Hattie would put it, "Turn over my soul."

One afternoon I went to visit Hattie. I hadn't seen her in a long time and needed to talk to her. When I got there, she was sitting on the front porch, rocking back and forth in that old chair. I could tell she was happy to see me. She stared at me for a long time and said, "Honey, it's gonna be all right. I know you got sumethin on your mind real heavy. Whenever you ready to tell ole Hattie, I'll be right here to listen."

I smiled and said, "Hattie, everything is fine. How you been doing?"

Hattie smiled and said, "Girl, I am takin it one step at a time. God is good all the time."

She looked over at me and started telling me that people were talking about seeing me in church every Sunday and how I was praising the Lord. I never did tell Hattie about what happened to Jt. I could tell she knew something had happened. I thought about coming over here plenty of times but I didn't.

She looked over to me and said, "Alice, the Lord has a strange way of changin people's life. I guess it ain't too late for ya."

I smiled and said, "Well Hattie, I guess it ain't."

I went up on the porch and sat on the top step. She started talking, telling me about Pearlie. Talking about Pearlie and Staley seeing each other and living together. I didn't know if she was talking to me or to herself.

She looked over to me and said, "Lord, where's my manners? Girl gon on in there and get you sumthin to drink. Get up off dem steps and come and sit over here."

She pointed to the chair on the side of her. I got up off the steps and sat down in the chair.

"Thanks Hattie, but I don't want anything to drink. I'm all right."

She turned and stared at me for a long time like she wanted to ask or tell me something. I just stared back at her waiting for what she wanted to ask me. She turned back around and started talking again in a low whisper.

"I am sho happy to see ya. Do you know my sister has finally got a man down there after all these years? Lord, you know that woman has been without a man for too long. I know she's puttin a hurtin on him in the bedroom. I know she's bout to kill him. Every time I see Staley, he got a big grin on his face like a chest cat. They both seem to be happy tho."

I started laughing, and looked over to Hattie and said, "Girl you know you're crazy. Your mind is still in the wrong place. Hattie, you ain't changed a bit."

We were laughing when all of a sudden Hattie just stopped. She had this serious look on her face like she was caught by surprise. She got really quiet, and then she started talking about Josiah. Telling me what type of man he was, how they met and how mean he had gotten once his eye was knocked out.

She looked over to me and said, "Girl, I loved me some Josiah. If I didn't think I had killed him, I would still be with him today. I probably would have ended up killin him later anyway, because he was gettin meaner than a rattlin snake."

Hattie started laughing at herself for what she had just said, which to me wasn't funny in no way. I knew Hattie could take a life and think nothing of it. She was telling me about their whole life together. I just sat there and listened to her talk.

She turned towards me and said, "If I ever wondered across his path again, I would ask him for his forgiveness. It ain't like I meant to leave him there for dead, I just didn't meant to. Didn't know what else to do. Just thought I had killed him and knew I had to get away before the law got on me."

Hattie turned away from me and stared out into the distant, rocking back and forth and being quiet in deep thought. She started rocking and humming all calm like.

"You know Alice, I have don a lot of things in my life that I am ashamed of. At the time I didn't know what I was doin. I just wanted to be loved, that's all. If I could turn back the hands of time, I would do it in a minute. I know it just ain't right to take another person's life away from em, it just ain't right. That should be the Lord's doin, not man. I prayed and ask the Lord to forgive me for my mean ways and the things I've don in my past. Like I said I just wanted to be loved. But didn't know how to ask for it."

She looked over at me and smiled.

"Alice, you're a good person, you've been a good friend."

She placed her hands over on top of mine and held her head down like she was prayin and said, "Lord, I thank you for the hard times and I thank you for the good ones. Thank you for teachin my friend and me how to turn over our soul. We are better people because of it. Lord, we have been through a lot and we are still here. Thank you Lord."

I looked over to Hattie and was wondering where all this was comin from. This was the first time I have ever seen or heard her pray. I've never seen this side of her. I guess she was asking for forgiveness in her own way.

She let go of my hand and started talking about the Juke-Joint. I knew Hattie was strange. She looked over to me and said, "Friendship last forever Alice, but men come and go. Look at us. Neither one of us got a man, but we're still here."

She started to laugh like it was really funny. Tears started to come to my eyes because while she was praying, I was thinking about Jt.

I turned to Hattie and said, "Hattie, I want to tell you something. You gonna have to promise me you gonna listen to what I have to say and know I am telling you the truth."

She had this strange look on her face.

"Alice, you know you can talk to me about anything."

I held my breath and started telling Hattie everything about Jt. About how I met him and how he didn't want anybody to know he was here and what happened to him. I started from the first day we met till the last day he was killed. I couldn't believe I was telling her this.

She just sat there rocking and not saying a word. I looked over at her and she seemed to be in another place. I didn't know If she was listening to me or not. I had to stop and ask her a couple of times if she was hearing me.

She would look over to me and say, "I hear you just fine baby."

I continued to tell her everything. I made sure I told her I didn't put two and two together about who Jt was until after she had gotten hurt.

I finished my story and just sat there waiting for Hattie to say something but she never did. I looked over at her and she still had this look on her face. She didn't look surprised or anything. She just looked calm.

I turned to her and said, "Hattie, have you heard anything I've said?"

She looked over to me.

"Alice baby, I've heard every word you said."

I turned away from Hattie and looked out over the field and notice how beautiful the sun was. I realized that Hattie had changed a lot since she had gotten out of the hospital.

I started thinking about my life. I had really made a lot of changes and was trying to do the right thing. I wondered how Hattie would feel if she knew I had planned on taking her life. Nobody had ever put it together that it was me who hire Ruthie Mae to kill Hattie, not even Hattie. I wanted her dead. I don't think she even knew it was my husband she had killed. The only reason I came back here was to get revenge on her. Everybody around town thought it was a man, but naw it was me. I hated Hattie for killing my man. That was the first person I had ever love. I had to let go of that hatred. I knew I couldn't get to heaven with my heart filled like that.

Hattie looked over to me and said, "Alice, life has a strange way of workin itself out. Lord knows, I'm glad I turned over my soul before it got too late."

After she said that, she looked back out into the distant and never said a word about what I had just told her. I didn't know where Hattie's mind was, but I did know, it was in a better place. I was thinking, "Yea Hattie, I guess you right."

978-0-595-36941-6
0-595-36941-3